G·r·e·a·t W·i·t·s

. . . .

Great

William Morrow and Company, Inc.
New York

. . . .

W·i·t·s

Alice Mattison

The following stories have appeared in *The New Yorker:* "Bears,"
"The Knitting," "New Haven," "In Family," "The Middle Ages,"
"They All Went Up to Amsterdam," and "Great Wits."
"Painting Day" appeared in *Fiction Network.*

Library of Congress Cataloging-in-Publication Data

Mattison, Alice.
   Great wits.
   I. Title.
PS3563.A8598G7   1988   813'.54   88-1666
ISBN 0-688-08060-X

Printed in the United States of America

First Edition

1 2 3 4 5 6 7 8 9 10

BOOK DESIGN BY DALE COTTON

For Edward

Contents

G·r·e·a·t W·i·t·s

Bears

My friend Pauline and I were talking, and she told me about a day she once spent in the country with a lover—how they parked at the side of a road and entered a chilly woods, then came upon an old apple orchard, warm in the sun, where they made love. She said that in that memory she sees her entire self, sees the two of them walk toward the woods as if from the viewpoint of someone facing them—herself in a blue jacket, her hands in the pockets, her face enlivened by some argument she's making.

I objected. I said my memories don't work that way at all, that they're seen from *within*. In important ones—the first time Louis and I kissed, for instance—I always remember just what I heard and saw originally, the appropriate and the incongruous mixed: in the case of the kiss, his wiry dark hair (as in a landscape seen through a network of branches and twigs, because there's a bare tree in the foreground) across the window (behind him) of the art room in the day-care center; then the stained concrete well of the window farther off, and, back inside, orange plastic cups on the sill, full of drying paint-brushes, their soft, trim heads, of different widths, watching us like little interested furry creatures.

I told Pauline that my memories were never like hers, but then, the next day, I found myself just humming a memory along—if you understand what I mean—and then I noticed that in it, sure enough, I am the person being looked at, as if I'm watching a film of myself. There's hair in this one too. I have long blond hair—a darkish blond, not beautiful but tangled and bushy; my daughters have the same hair, though finer and brighter, because they are children. The memory is of the winter four years ago, when Hilary was nine and Susannah was a year and a half old and was starting at the day-care cooperative. I'd been separated from Carl for a while by then. In the memory, I am about to take Susannah home. It's five o'clock, dark outside, and around us is the mild turmoil of parents sorting out their children's belongings and finding their boots. I am facing into the main room of the day-care center, ready to roll—a big purse on my shoulder, Susannah's fuzzy green blanket under one elbow, and Susannah herself in my arms. She can walk but she is still clumsy, especially in snow. I look short in my wide, puffy gray-and-pink jacket, woven in zig-zags. I'm holding Susannah under her arms, her face to mine, and she's in a dark- and light-blue print snowsuit with the hood (which she hates) still down, and pink quilted boots. What you also see of us, along with the two kinds of blond hair and the two kinds of coat, is my forehead (it looks conscientious) above her head, and my car keys already dangling from one of my hands, which is grasping my other hand across Susannah's back. In a moment I will turn and head stalwartly for the door and out into the cold with my big baby, but now I look over Susannah's head at nothing, or at you, the viewer, and I see, examining the memory, that "you" are Louis, the head teacher, the only person still in indoor clothing, who is watching the children with whom he's spent his day being squashed back into the lumpy, complicated shapes—part child, part parent—that bundled themselves in here way back in the morning. When we are gone, Louis will feel the new silence settle around his ears, then walk through it, put on his own brown jacket, lock up, and go home.

Louis had been a student in the art school at Yale, and when he graduated he'd applied for the job at the cooperative, saying he wanted to stay in New Haven. He'd always wanted to work with kids, and he couldn't sell paintings anyway. When my old friend Pauline started urging me to send Susannah to the cooperative day-care center where her daughter went, she promised that I'd like Louis Feingold. "He's always down on the rug with the kids, stretched out on his stomach," she said. "When I come in, he gets up on one elbow to talk to me. He wears sweaters. He's got lots of wild Jewish hair. He looks like my cousin."

I did like Louis, but I was busy that winter, just keeping track. I had a new job, Hilary spent her afternoons at the houses of three different friends, and on Wednesday afternoons I had to take my turn staffing the day-care center, which meant a special arrangement at work. I was always making a list—and then, with satisfaction, crossing the items out.

One Wednesday we took the whole group to the park two blocks away. We were a gallant caravan; we had a big stroller for Susannah and another baby, and a yellow wooden wagon for three two-year-olds. The bigger children held on to a frayed clothesline to keep together. Winding slowly along, we made it to the playground, and the kids scattered. There was a father there that day, Don, who stayed near the slide, catching people who came down too fast, and a volunteer from Yale, Lisa, who watched over children on the climbing equipment. Louis and I put six kids into the baby swings, all in a row at the top of the hill, and then stood behind them, giving a push here and there.

It was a windy day in, I think, late February, but the wind was warm, with a loamy smell. The snow was mostly gone and the ground wasn't too wet. It wasn't pretty in the park. It was a brown, rumpled part of the year, with a few withered leaves still on the trees—just veins of leaves, really—but I was exhilarated. I liked not being at work but not being the sole adult at home, either. I wasn't cold, for once. I unzipped my jacket and ran up and down the line of swings, giving a shove to each seat just as it swung back to me, like someone playing a song by tapping Coke bottles. The children laughed.

Louis, who had a woolen muffler around his neck but wasn't wearing a coat, pumped his arms to keep warm. Someone knitted for him, I thought. His heavy sweater with cables up and down it looked handmade, like the scarf. It was brown, with tiny flecks of color.

"I needed my coat after all," he said. "I'm like the kids. The first *really* warm day, I'll take it off somewhere and lose it."

"I'm always piling on sweaters," I said, "just in case."

"You know how if you go into Clark's Dairy in June, there's always one scarf on the coatrack, all gray and grungy?" He poked his chest solemnly. "My scarf. Oh, I'll be right back."

I watched him as he loped down the hill—Stephen had fallen off some wooden steps, and Lisa had picked him up. Louis helped her brush Stephen off, and then picked him up for a minute, said something to Lisa, who laughed, and put him down again. Louis's muffler, which had been tucked in, came loose as he trotted back up the hill. "I wish Thursdays were like Wednesdays," he said, winding it around his neck. He walked to the front of the swings and pulled each child forward in turn, up high, and then let go.

"What's wrong with Thursdays?"

"It's not the same," he said. "The parents who work then, Jean and Kathy—well, Jean's a little spacy and Kathy's nervous. And there's no volunteer."

"Maybe you should move Lisa," I said.

"No, I asked her. She can't. Nobody can change." He grabbed Susannah's legs and backed up as far as he could with her, then let go of the swing. "If we came here on a Thursday," he said, "Jean would wander into the woods and be eaten by wild beasts." He moved off about ten feet down the hill and called out, "Hey, guys, we should head back in a couple of minutes!"

I looked to see whether the children had heard what was going to happen to Jean, but they weren't paying attention. We began lifting them out of the swings, and then we started back, with Louis coming last, pushing the stroller, and me a little way ahead with three bigger kids. Lisa and the wagon were ahead of me, and Don was holding the front end of the rope, taking big, slow steps and singing in a cracked voice, "Here we go back to *day* care, all on a winter's day!" He's an economics professor at Southern Connecticut.

I tried to remember to walk slowly enough so as not to get ahead of the children, and thought about first learning that walk when Hilary was little. Then it occurred to me that maybe Hilary could be of use to Louis if she came after school on Thursdays. I waited until we were inside the yard and then let Louis catch up, and asked him about it, a little hesitantly. "She's nine," I explained. "She's good with little kids. She could read stories."

He was leaning over the stroller, lifting the babies out, but he straightened up, beaming. "Carolyn, you're a genius," he said. Then he stepped back, as if he needed room, and hugged me—not a personal hug but a public, ceremonial one. His arms went straight out and he held them that way for a second, then stepped forward and wrapped them swiftly around me, as if what I'd said (though I didn't think it was *that* bright) were so smart that I had to be hugged, as if hugs were medals.

I was laughing, of course, but something made me turn away quickly and pick up Susannah. Then, as we pushed the stroller and herded the children back into the building, I saw that it was the remarkable amplitude of my delight at what he'd done that made me shy.

Still, we didn't become lovers until May. Hilary went to day care, gladly, every Thursday, and taught songs to the three- and four-year-olds; Louis told me she made a big difference. On Wednesdays, we went to the park more often. I was awkward with Louis, though—I was thinking about him a good deal, I noticed—but then I saw that he was the same, and I thought I knew what would happen one day when Carl had taken Hilary and Susannah overnight and I agreed to meet Louis at five and help him straighten up the art supplies.

Then I decided I'd been wrong, because as we worked, sorting the children's paintings, he told me about a woman he'd loved—"Mary Elizabeth," he said slowly, with a tiny pause between the names—who was married. He'd known her for two years; she'd been an art student with him, and they used to take anguished coffee breaks together. When Louis told me this, I thought that he just wanted me for a confidante, and the art room looked less colorful as I made silent plans about how to comfort myself when I was alone. I'd start reading a new book I'd bought, and take a bath, and call Pauline. . . .

But Louis, who was standing on a low chair taping a finger painting to the wall with masking tape, went on talking. "It's different now," he said, and stepped down and stood back to admire the painting, which showed a face outlined in orange with a shaggy sunburst all around it. It could have been an animate sun, I thought, or possibly a man with a beard. "You can't lie to yourself around kids," he said. "Probably it's always been a fantasy."

Now I understood that, in telling me about Mary Elizabeth, Louis had been engaging in full disclosure, as I think the Truth-in-Lending statute calls it. We put all the scissors into one cigar box, and cleaned the paintbrushes, and then, at last, got around to kissing.

It was good, being with Louis. He'd come over and we'd care for the children together, or I'd get a sitter and we'd go to his apartment for the evening. By August he was sleeping over at my place several nights a week, and we were talking about living together. Then the children and I spent a weekend with him at his parents' summer cottage in the Adirondacks.

All I had known about Mr. and Mrs. Feingold, before we went, was that his mother knitted his scarves and sweaters. I had been worried that they'd disapprove of me—Hilary was sometimes rude, Susannah wasn't toilet trained, we're not Jewish—though Louis kept telling me that they wouldn't be whatever I'd been picturing. Actually, his father was exactly as I'd imagined him, except that he couldn't resist children, and he was trading riddles with Hilary moments after we arrived. Louis's mother matter-of-factly assigned Louis and me to a double bed—something else I'd worried about—and quickly told me that she only knitted between books. She was a translator, it turned out, who worked on technical books in German and Dutch.

She glared at me briefly when I complimented her on her knitting, as if she'd caught me hoping for a sweater during the book season, and then told me about her current project, a Dutch entomology textbook. "I don't suppose you know Dutch?" she said, but then shook her head firmly when I said no. "Of course not—just because you're blond. It would be too much to expect."

We were outside their cottage, being shown the lake, admiring the mountains, dark with evergreens. "At first I was leery about this book," said Miriam Feingold. "You know, the Netherlands—so damp. I thought they'd have disgusting insects, like centipedes. Every book I translate comes into my dreams. But it's mostly anatomy, and it doesn't have to do with Dutch insects in particular. Now that I think about it, I can't imagine *any* bugs in Holland. It doesn't seem like a buggy place at all." As she spoke, she was yanking beach towels off the clothesline and draping them, folded once lengthwise, over her left arm. "You wouldn't know, would you?"

Again I had to say no. Miriam looked a little disappointed. She also seemed puzzled when she learned that I'm a paralegal but that I don't want to go to law school, though Louis's unambitious life seemed to delight her. Nonetheless, I saw that she was a person you could argue with, and we made friends. Only one bad thing happened that weekend. The second evening, we were all outside the house after supper—there was a little lawn, with a few chairs—and suddenly Hilary seized Susannah's hand and ran across the road with her in the twilight, without looking. She must have forgotten it wasn't a driveway but a real road, though with little traffic. A car was coming, in fact, but it was far away, and the children were never in danger. I wasn't too upset—I was more concerned that Hilary would be embarrassed at her mistake—but Louis, who'd raced across after them and held their hands until the car had passed, couldn't seem to forget the incident. At breakfast he said, "Hill, I'm sorry, but I need to talk about you know what—last night—again."

"I *did* look," said Hilary.

"I wish you didn't need to see it that way," said Louis. "Nobody's angry. You were a little out of control. It happens to me too." He pushed his chair back and stood up, holding his coffee mug, pausing on the way to the stove. "I guess it bothers me because you had Susannah. Damn it, Hill, all I want is to talk about how scared *I* am, at times—you know, being the person in charge of little kids."

His father, who had walked into town for the *Times* early in the morning, now raised his head from it, his coffee mug to his lips, and looked out at us from under his hair—all over the place, like his son's hair, but gray and thinner.

"I take good care of my sister," said Hilary.

"Louis, lay off it," I said. "She's *nine*."

"You're right," said Louis. "She's so good on Thursday afternoons I forget she isn't twenty."

That helped. "I'm glad Louis met you," Miriam said to me later, as we came back from a walk. She'd shown me some blackberry bushes in a sunny place along the road, and we'd filled a saucepan, reaching across the bristly canes for the best berries, the big shiny ones. "I hope you're not too smart for him," she said.

"Louis is smart!" I said, shocked.

"Of course," said Miriam.

Louis came to my house in the brown cable-knit sweater on a cold, rainy Sunday evening in late September. My kitchen was warm and steamy, for I'd been cooking—reveling in cooking, because it was the first day cold enough to hover around the stove. He began pulling the sweater up over his head as he followed me in. I hadn't seen him for a few days. He'd been painting, and I'd had to bring work home from the office. He kissed me more passionately than he usually did on nights the children were home. Then he put the sweater down on the nearest chair and sat down heavily on the next one, which was odd—usually he stood near me and talked for a few minutes while I cooked, and then he tore lettuce or scraped carrots. I had stewed a chicken and now I was breaking green beans to put into the pot. He didn't say anything for a minute, and then he said, "Tropical rain forest in here." I had spider plants in front of both kitchen windows, and the windows were fogged up. "Is everything all right?" he said then.

"Sure," I said. "I had a good day. I did laundry, and I baked gingerbread. I can't remember whether you like gingerbread."

"Sure I do," he said. Then he said, "Carolyn, there are some things I need to talk about," and that sounded bad, but just then Susannah came groggily into the kitchen, her face red and damp, with one strap of her overalls dangling down her back. She'd fallen asleep on the living-room rug at five, and late naps made her cranky. I picked her up and held her on my hip, trying to do the beans with my free hand, but she cried, and finally I lowered the flame under the chicken and sat down to button her overalls and cuddle her. "Start some rice, would you?" I said to Louis.

The doorbell rang. Louis went to answer it with the box of rice in his hand, and it was Hilary, who'd been across the street at a friend's. She followed him back in, talking, and he cooked the rice while Susannah calmed down, and then we ate, but he and I weren't alone again until supper was over and the children were in bed. Finally I came out of their room. Louis was washing the dishes. All evening, of course, I'd been trying to imagine what he would say, and I'd decided the likeliest thing was that he wanted to quit his day-care job. That would be upsetting, because we saw each other there a lot, and it would be bad news for Susannah and the other children. But while I was giving Susannah her bath, I realized that this possibility wasn't bad enough. After all, if Louis left day care we could still see each other—we could live together, in fact; he'd said he didn't think it would be good for him *or* Susannah to be together twenty-four hours a day, and so he and I had renewed our separate leases. It must be that he was quitting and leaving New Haven, I concluded—that *would* be bad.

"I don't know if I was ever straight with you, Carolyn," he said now, turning away from the sink. I sat down at the kitchen table. The yellow paper napkins we'd used were still there, and I began tearing the one in front of me, making a fringe around its edge. Louis leaned on the sink. He had a cup of coffee and every now and then he took a sip. I began to hurt inside.

"I know I tried to explain to you," he said, "that there had been somebody else . . ." He paused, and I nodded quickly, like a child who's being told bad news and pretends it isn't getting to him.

Then he was quiet for a time, and then he said, "Mary Elizabeth called me."

"When?" I said.

"Last week," he said. "Maybe two weeks ago. Two weeks ago at the most."

"What did she want?"

"Well," he said. "Well, it's not that she wanted something. It's not that. It's just . . . Well, she's thinking about leaving Tom."

"Louis—" I said. "I can't believe this. You come here and tell me that Mary Elizabeth is thinking of leaving Tom?" I started to cry. "What's that to us?"

"Nothing," he said quickly. "Nothing. I mean, I *think* nothing. Very likely nothing. But Carolyn, I have to sort this out, don't I?"

I said, "Louis, are you breaking up with me?"

"No," he said. "I'm not. Well, maybe. I just think we need some sort of change until I figure this out. Oh, Carolyn, I'm still not being straight with you." He turned from the sink, leaving the remaining dishes, and walked to the window with his coffee cup and looked out at the darkness. He must have seen nothing there but his own reflection through the fronds of the spider plant.

"I'd have sworn it wouldn't matter who called me up," he said. "I wasn't thinking about her. And then, when she did— well, it was a big thing. I . . . I saw her, last week. I'm sorry. It scared me. I'm scared."

I wasn't going to ask whether they'd slept together, because I knew he'd tell me the truth. Besides, to say it would be to imagine it. "There's no Mary Elizabeth!" I shouted. "I don't believe in her. There *is* no Mary Elizabeth."

"I'm afraid there is," he said, turning around. I cried, and he came up behind me, put the cup down, and held my shoulders, and then I got up and walked into the living room. I didn't want to talk about it anymore until I'd had a chance to be alone, but he sat down, so I took off my shoes and sat down on the sofa. Then he got up and sat down again, and then he said, "Did Pauline tell you what happened Thursday?"

It seemed a strange time to talk about Pauline or Thursday. "No," I said. "I haven't talked to Pauline all weekend."

"I thought you must know about it and be mad at me."

"What do you mean?" I said. I tried to remember what the

current day-care hassle was—there was always something—but I was too upset to care. I was cold, too. My feet were cold, so I sat on them.

"I didn't see it," he said, "which was negligent. Pauline's angry with me and she's right."

"Pauline's angry with you?"

"I'm sure this will come up at a meeting," he said. "But the main thing is, it has to do with Hilary."

"What *happened*?" I said.

"Well, of course Hilary was at day care on Thursday," he said. "And Rita came to pick up Josh a little early." Josh was a four-year-old who'd recently joined. Rita, his mother, was a hardworking member—she'd made curtains for the nap room— but she was a little *too* energetic, I sometimes thought.

"Apparently she saw Josh in the reading corner with Heather and Stephen and Jessica—all the four-year-olds. Hilary was telling them stories. And as Rita heads over there Pauline comes in and they stop to talk, but I guess they can hear Hilary, and she's making up *horror* stories—about kids with their names getting captured, I think by wild animals. And the kids are looking nervous. So Rita bawled out Hilary and told the kids not to pet strange dogs or something. And Pauline found me— I was in the art room, cleaning up—and gave me hell. For not checking. I don't know. I'm surprised Hilary would do that. She must have felt terrible when Rita yelled at her. But do you think she's—I don't know—troubled? To focus on violence like that? And the kids—I'd hate to have Rita and the rest yank their kids out. I've been worried about this all weekend." He stood up and sat down again. "I was sure Pauline came straight over here and said something."

I almost laughed at the thought of Rita, whom, I decided, I didn't like, discovering what was going on, but I told myself wearily that I shouldn't make light of it, that Louis thought it was important. I'd caught Hilary scaring Susannah once with a story about a wolf, but it hadn't occurred to me that she'd try it at day care. Still, I was so upset already that after telling myself I'd talk to Hilary—and Rita and Pauline—I forgot about it.

"Louis broke up with me," I said the next evening, as soon as Pauline and I were alone in her kitchen. I'd called her at her office and said I needed to come over later; I could stand it, I thought, if I could talk about it. Now Susannah was playing with Pauline's daughter, Iris, and Hilary was on the living-room rug doing homework and eating a carrot. Pauline was standing at the stove scooting chopped meat and onions around in a pan for spaghetti sauce, and I was watching her.

"I don't believe it," she said.

I told her what had happened. She kept looking at me and shaking her head. "I even hate her *name*," I finished. "Nobody's called 'Mary Elizabeth' anyway. If she were a reasonable human being, wouldn't it at least be 'Mary Beth'?"

"Of course," said Pauline.

"Or it would be slurred," I said. "He says it so clearly, as if it's so *important*."

I cried then, and she put her arm around me and gave me a glass of wine and invited us all to stay for supper. "I didn't think this would happen," she said. "I like Louis. I thought he was a grown-up."

That made me remember the last part of my conversation with him. "He says you're mad at him."

"Well, of course."

"No—I forgot. He says you're mad because Hilary scared the four-year-olds."

"Oh, *that*," she said. "I thought I'd wait for the principals to tell you before I did, and then I just forgot about it."

"Well, Hilary hasn't said a word," I said. "And Louis was a little garbled."

"This may cause a minor uproar at day care," said Pauline. "Rita put it on the agenda for the meeting, but I thought it was funny. Here's this winning little scene, with Hilary spinning yarns"—she lowered her voice—"and suddenly I hear her clearly and she's saying, 'So the giant ate up Josh's arms and legs, and the bear had the rest of him.' "

I laughed, though my face was still wet from crying. Then I said, "Were the kids upset?"

"Actually, I think they liked it. They were probably more worried by Rita's lecture. I really lost it, though. Rita was blaming Hilary—the worst of this is that Rita yelled at Hilary—and I got mad at Rita, and mad at *Louis* for letting Hilary get into trouble. That's farfetched, but I let him have it. You know me. I'd call him and apologize, but not now."

"Pauline," I said, "do you think there's something wrong with Hilary—that she'd do it? Do I have to pack away my broken heart and worry about my kid?"

"No," said Pauline. "Kids say things. Louis has been expecting too much of her."

"He thinks she's an adult." I remembered what happened at his parents' place. "I guess he's upset."

"He didn't know what to do when I yelled at him," said Pauline. "He was washing the art-room floor. He had that huge mop with the strings going in every direction, and he looked as if he'd been snared in it. Oh!" She turned around. "Carolyn!"

"What?"

"Is this my fault, for yelling at him? Do you think he broke up with you out of *embarrassment*?"

I couldn't help it, I laughed. "Were you very fierce?" I said. I'd been yelled at by Pauline once or twice, and I knew how it felt.

"Pretty fierce, but he *knows* me."

I remembered Louis saying he was scared, Sunday night, but he'd said it, of course, about Mary Elizabeth. I didn't know whether Louis was the sort of person who could be scared away by—by just *things,* the things that happen. "Maybe he thinks if he hangs around me and my kids the bears will get *him,*" I said. I didn't know—but of course it was Mary Elizabeth I was thinking about. About her and about how I'd have to work my turn with Louis on Wednesday, and how the bottom drawer of my dresser was filled with his socks and underwear and a shirt and a pair of pajamas. Sometimes, these months, I'd forgotten and opened it, looking for the sweaters I used to keep in it before I knew Louis, and I'd always liked that— being stopped, especially on the mornings he wasn't there (behind me, naked from the shower, reaching for his own clothes), by his possessions, which all seemed right for him: the ordinary tan pajamas, frayed at the wrists, as if he'd somehow found pajamas that had his name, or his message, all over them.

In the next weeks, everything gave me trouble: dropping off Susannah or picking her up, seeing Louis at day care, or not seeing him. I managed to change my arrangement at work so I could be at day care on Monday mornings, when Louis taught a painting class at Albertus Magnus College and didn't come. We saw each other, and he even came to dinner now and then, but it seemed we weren't supposed to sleep together until he'd figured out how he felt about Mary Elizabeth—or until *she* figured out how she felt about Tom. It also appeared that I wasn't supposed to ask questions. He'd hold me by the upper arms and kiss me sorrowfully.

I didn't attend the day-care meeting at which Hilary's scary story was discussed, but, according to Pauline, nothing much happened. Rita was still angry. Everyone tried to reassure her, and Louis apologetically agreed he should supervise Hilary more closely, and then offered to take the children to look at the chipmunks and raccoons at the West Rock Nature Center, so they wouldn't be afraid of animals. "They make up scary stories all the time, on their own," someone pointed out. Hilary never would talk about what had happened, though nobody blamed her and everyone told her they were glad she worked at day care. A few weeks later, though, she said she wanted to take drama after school, and the class met on Thursdays, so that was that. "I helped enough," she said.

"*Has* Mary Elizabeth left Tom?" I said once, to Pauline. "You'd think I could know that much."

"We could call her up and ask her."

"I don't know her last name," I said.

"How about a personal ad? There must be people who know all about it. 'Can anyone tell us whether Mary Elizabeth has left Tom?' "

"Don't you know any artists?" I said. "And don't all artists know all *other* artists?"

Pauline is a social worker, but she has all sorts of friends. "I know musicians," she said thoughtfully. "I know a potter. . . . Let me think about it."

In November I got a phone call from Miriam Feingold. "I want you to trace your children's hands," she said. I had a sudden leap of the heart: a love charm!—but no, she was between books and was knitting mittens for Hilary and Susannah. "For Christmas," she said. "Hanukkah. Whatever."

I thanked her.

"I'm sorry about you and Louis," she said, "but I refuse to pretend I don't know you. Sometimes I think that's what the men I know are *for*—to introduce me to interesting women, whom they then ditch. Though I didn't expect it of Louis."

I was pleased to hear that I was interesting.

"Don't give up on him," she went on. "You know, that's just what I used to say to his teachers. But it's true. Eventually, he pulls things together."

"Do you *think* so?" I said, but she turned apologetic.

"Oh, I know, I'm his mother. Don't listen to *me*," she said.

It was hard to persuade Susannah to have her hand traced, but Hilary was interested, and at last Susannah, too, lowered her palm warily onto the paper. At first I outlined their hands with the fingers spread, and it was lovely guiding the pencil past each joint of each of their fingers. After I'd drawn in their nails and the little lines on their knuckles, I realized that of course Miriam only needed tracings with the fingers together and the thumbs out, mitten style, so I had to persuade Susannah all over again. The hands were on one big sheet of paper, and I found a big envelope and sent the whole thing off to her. A few weeks later, the mittens came—purple with lavender thumbs for Hilary, and lavender with purple thumbs for Susannah. Miriam had also made me a vest, in a gray-blue yarn that frizzled all over into a soft cloud. I wore it, under or on top of another sweater, all winter—a hard winter for me—even though I looked fat in so many layers.

One Friday in February the day care held a potluck supper at Don and Marjorie's house. I always made myself go to gatherings like that, whether Louis went or not, so I signed up to bring a dessert, and, the night before, I baked brownies. Don and Marjorie's house is small, and it was crowded when I arrived. I made my way through the group with my pan of brownies and my daughters, and we found a place to put our coats and then filled our paper plates with lasagna and salad. In those days I was sensitive to Louis's presence, and from the moment we came in I had felt that he was in the dining room. Sure enough, he was talking to Don, leaning against a wall and eating. We passed them with our plates, and Louis stretched out a hand behind him, not turning his head, to touch my arm. We hadn't talked for a week—he'd started a conversation at five o'clock one day, when I was picking up Susannah, but a moment later someone called him away.

Pauline and another woman were in the living room, and I joined them. I was feeling bad and I didn't say anything, I just ate. They were discussing a membership drive we were planning, but then the other woman went back to the dining room for seconds.

"I know something," said Pauline to me at once, "but I don't know whether it's good or bad, so maybe you don't want to talk about it."

"Tell me," I said.

"I know about Mary Elizabeth and Tom," she said. "It turns out that Tom is a social worker. He works for the state. I even *know* him. I mean, he's one of a couple of guys in that office I always mix up."

"How do you know Tom is the right Tom?" I said.

"A woman in my office—Karen—wants his job," she said. "His last name is Frederick. Karen told me Tom Frederick may move to New Jersey, because his wife, an artist, is already down there, and I immediately although discreetly asked her name, and it's the same woman. It's her."

"So she did leave him."

"She left him. She moved to New Jersey, but . . . Well, Karen said there was somebody else, who was here."

Now I got scared that Louis would move to New Jersey, but then I remembered that *Tom* was moving to New Jersey.

"But they're getting back together?" I said.

"According to Karen, they're not sure. I didn't like the sound of them, frankly. Wishy-washy. As if they'll never settle it."

"But he's moving down there?"

"Probably."

"You mean she hasn't been in New Haven for *months*?"

I'd been afraid of meeting her everywhere. Once, I'd been convinced—for no reason—that a woman ahead of me in the dentist's waiting room, who looked arty and confident, was Mary Elizabeth, and then I'd been cheerful all day after the hygienist stuck her head out and called her Jennifer.

Now Don came around with a jug of Burgundy and poured some into our paper cups. Pauline and I toasted Mary Elizabeth and Tom's marriage, and then we toasted Karen's new job, but I was faking my glee a little, because New Jersey wasn't far enough away.

"Did you see the drawings?" said Louis then, marching up to Pauline and me—we'd changed the subject not a moment too soon. "In the art room. They take up every inch of wall."

The drawings, he said, were life-size outlines of the children themselves. He'd gotten hold of a huge roll of butcher paper, and the children had taken turns lying down on it while other children crawled around them, tracing around their bodies. Then they colored in the faces, hair, and clothes.

"Wait till you see Susannah's," he said to me.

"Did she *let* you?" I asked. "I traced her hand, and she was afraid."

"It was hard," he said. "Two-year-olds think it's magic—if you trace them, you *get* them. But she was all right. Maybe now that she's a little older . . ."

I hadn't said how long ago I had traced Susannah's hand, and I wondered whether he knew about it.

"Besides, I was the first victim," he went on. "I lay down and let them trace me." He held his arms and legs a little out, like a gingerbread man. "It was strange," he said. "I lay there looking up at the ceiling of the art room, trying not to move, and all their crayons kept tickling me here and there—their hands were holding me still, all up and down me. And then do you know what they did? They colored me in naked."

"They *did?*" said Pauline, with a laugh. I had stopped worrying about New Jersey and was interested.

"Of course it didn't matter with my face," said Louis, "but they gave me a regular *forest* of chest hair, and a belly button, and pubic hair yet, and a penis."

"Did they draw themselves naked?" said Pauline.

"No, only me. They couldn't make long lines, so my outline is a million tiny lines in different colors—a red hand and an orange arm, but my hair is brown. I look shaggy and I'm very large—I take up the whole wall opposite the doorway. I look like an abominable snowman or a brown bear, but I have a big smile."

"I can't wait to see this," said Pauline.

"Oh, but listen to what happened then," said Louis. "Rita came to get Josh, and she came into the art room and admired everything, and then she took me aside and very seriously said to me, 'Louis, you didn't *pose* like that, did you?' "

"Oh, that's wonderful," I said. "What did you answer?"

"This is terrible," said Louis. "I told her I did."

Pauline and I laughed, but Louis said, "That was bad." And

then he looked across the room to where Rita was talking with a group of people and drinking wine. She wasn't far away at all, but Louis rested one hand on my shoulder and one hand on Pauline's, rose up on tiptoe, and then raised the hand that had been on Pauline's shoulder. "Rita!" he called. And as he did it (his other hand still touching me) I felt something become new, though I don't know why. It was like watching a movie when the projectionist brings it into sharper focus. Suddenly, everything is a little less fuzzy, while voices are a bit more distinct, though a moment later you can't say what has been altered. A woman named Jane was coming toward us and smiling, and someone behind us was calling, "Dessert!," and I knew something, just then, about Louis—central Louis, that crisply drawn person (we each must have one) who's hardly ever visible through the blur. I knew Louis wasn't a silly man who loved Mary Elizabeth but a sensible man who loved me.

Rita turned around, looking anxious. "Rita!" said Louis. "I lied! I lied! I'm sorry." Then he sank back on his heels, and his voice, which had been a little antic, became lower and more natural. "I really *am* sorry."

She stared, and then she understood and laughed. I liked her for the first time—for not pretending to understand until she did. She turned away, blushing slightly, and turned back and called in a friendly voice, "I *thought* you might be making it up."

Louis turned back to us, took his hand off my shoulder, and, as if he'd been trying to work the information in somewhere but couldn't, said quickly to me—I remember myself standing there, a short blond woman squeezed between him and Pauline, holding a paper cup of red wine, wearing a blue vest—"I found the pictures of your children's hands, in my parents' apartment. I kept them."

The Knitting

Beth does not see, in time, the damp leaves on the sidewalk in front of her. She twists the bike to avoid them and loses her balance. It skids and falls, but slowly. She sinks sideways into a hedge. The twigs burn her hand and her bare ankles, but she is almost supported by the hedge as she goes down. She turns her face away, but scrapes the back of her leg on one pedal as she falls.

Her nephews come running from behind. Their feet sound louder in the twilight. They make a great show of helping her up and asking her if she has broken anything. She has not, nor is the hedge dented. A few twigs are broken. But she is scratched. It is getting dark.

"You can't stop now," says Philip, the older boy. "Like riding a horse . . ."

"I'm not frightened. I'm tired, though. And cold. In fact, I need to be with your mother."

"You can ride the bike home," Martin, the younger boy, says. They are five blocks away.

"I'd rather walk, really, if you don't mind bringing it," Beth says.

Martin mounts the bike and leads them toward the house. He rides slowly, not to get ahead of them, back and forth on the sidewalk. The bike leans when he curves to each side, but he does not fall off.

"Will you buy yourself a bike now?" Philip asks.

"Maybe," says Beth. "But I'd have to keep it in the apartment."

"How come you never learned to ride before?"

"I was waiting for you to grow up and teach me."

Her nephew laughs but then is silent. It isn't possible to know what he is feeling, or perhaps it is simply clearer with him than it was with Stephanie, the girl in the family—the oldest, now confined to a psychiatric hospital after an attempt at suicide—that personality is opaque. Beth did not learn to ride a bicycle as a child because when her sister Franny outgrew the littlest two-wheeler, their father put training wheels on it. Her friends had already learned to ride without training wheels; Beth was embarrassed. But why did she never learn as a teenager or an adult? Today, at lunch, she had mentioned idly that she couldn't ride a bicycle. Franny lent her a pair of jeans to be taught in. Her nephews brought Stephanie's ten-speed out of the basement, but when Beth protested they took it back and brought out Franny's old bike that she'd had since college. When her children were babies, Franny used to ride with one of them in the back, in a yellow plastic seat that is still gathering dust in the basement.

After an hour in the parking lot of the nearby high school, with Martin running patiently behind her, his hands out as if to catch a toddling baby, Beth could ride. Franny didn't think to lend her socks, and Beth had taken off her tights along with her skirt, afraid of tearing them.

When they reach the house, her brother-in-law Jack is standing outside. "They didn't take you out on Mitchell Drive, did they?" he says.

"No, we stayed on the sidewalk or on very quiet streets." The scratches on her ankles burn a little. She is about to help her nephews put the bike back in the basement when Franny comes to the door.

"Beth, there's a phone call for you."

"I'll be right back," she says to Philip and Martin. Franny is leaning against the porch railing; Jack has stopped at the bottom of the steps. They both keep looking out at the street as she walks past them.

The phone call is from Alec, the man she lives with in New York. He thinks she'd like to know about a letter that has come today. "It's from Agnes," he says. "Shouldn't I open it?" Agnes holds the lease to their apartment; originally she was Beth's roommate there. Alec is always afraid she will come back, or will decide to tell the landlord that she has handed the apartment on.

Beth doesn't want Alec to read her the letter. She wonders if he has already opened it. She has written to Agnes in detail about him. She tries to persuade him to put the letter aside, but when they hang up she is not sure he will.

Franny walks slowly into the kitchen, knitting. She is making an afghan. It will be made of eight strips, sewn together, of increasingly darker blues. She is working on a medium-blue strip. It hangs between her hands to her knees, swinging. She knits and walks, the cylindrical skein of yarn wedged under her right elbow. This stitch is a little complicated, so she must give each motion some attention. She walks slowly, not looking where she is going. She is wearing a corduroy back-wrap skirt and an old hand-knitted red pullover sweater. She is not much older than Beth but she looks older because she grew up early, and was used to makeup, hair waved at the hairdresser, and nylon stockings by the time Beth started college in the late sixties. Beth owns several formal suits, but she doesn't wear makeup on weekends.

This is the first time Beth has come to see her sister's family, here in New Haven, since Stephanie went into the hospital. On Sunday, the next day, she is to visit her niece, along with Franny. Only two visitors are permitted.

"I feel bad about taking the pass," says Beth. "Doesn't Jack want to go?"

"He went last week," Franny says. "Of course he'd like to, but he thinks it would be good for Steffie to see you. She's crazy about you, as everyone knows. And *she* wants it."

"Or the boys—"

"They're very awkward there. Martin's not really old enough. I lied once and said he was twelve, but he was angry. And I think it just upsets Philip to go. They're glad you're here. That's a help for them. Martin loved teaching you to ride the bike."

"I know."

Beth sits at the kitchen table. It's an old round oak table. The edge is battered. She runs her finger along the grain. She'd like to talk about her muted half-quarrels with Alec of the last weeks, but her sister does not ask about the phone call. Then Beth thinks they should talk about Stephanie. She would tell her sister not to blame herself, but she thinks Franny may not in fact be blaming herself—or, alternatively, perhaps she should be.

"Why *Steffie?*" she asks.

"I know. Yet I didn't feel surprised when I found her throwing up pills that morning."

"Why not?"

"I don't know why not. There's something in her that bypasses me. I've never been able to predict her."

"I found myself thinking that about Philip," says Beth.

"Oh, Philip. Philip's easy. I just look for myself in Philip. When he's silent, I can almost hear him counting, waiting until the point has been made, so he can talk again. Philip's always in dialogue."

What did she say, Beth wonders, that made Philip so quiet on the walk home?

"Franny, do you feel guilty?"

The phone rings. Franny picks up the receiver. "Hello? Hi, honey, how are you?" Then, "We're OK. Beth's here. . . . Well, yes—but that's not what you said, hon. . . ." Beth gets up. She goes upstairs to put on her skirt and tights. She is staying in Stephanie's room, instead of sleeping on the living-room couch, as she usually does. The room is neat, filled with photographs of modern dancers, art supplies, books. It could be the room of a happy person. When did she last see Stephanie? During her most recent visit, Stephanie was out baby-sitting much of the time. It has been a while since their traditional Christmas outings to *The Nutcracker.*

Beth leaves Franny's roomy jeans folded on the bed. Her feet are red and chilled. She works her tights up her legs, puts on her skirt, and combs her hair. When she comes down, Franny is off the phone, knitting at a chair pushed back from the kitchen table.

"My daughter."

"What?"

"Nothing serious, but this is embarrassing. She invited her friend Melissa to go see her tomorrow. She called to ask me to arrange to drive her. She says she just wants to see me for a few minutes, and then only Melissa."

Beth is pained. Has she been seeing herself as the person who would finally, easily, secure Stephanie's confidence? But she says, "That's OK. I mean, isn't it good that she wants to see her friends?"

"But we discussed the whole thing—in detail—last Sunday. Incredible detail. And she said she didn't want to see Melissa. She said Melissa's hostile."

There is some relief. It occurs to Beth, only now, that she has never visited a mental hospital. "I'll be up again—or maybe she'll be out soon."

Jack comes in. "Honey, she called," Franny says. "She doesn't want Beth to go see her. She wants me to take Melissa."

"What did you tell her?"

"What could I tell her? I said OK. She said she discussed it with her doctor. They agreed she needs to resolve some of the tensions between herself and her friends."

"All of a sudden, like this?"

"I'm not defending her. I think she just forgot Beth entirely."

Franny puts the afghan strip down on the table. Jack looks at Martin, who is coming into the kitchen, as if he wants to ask him something, but Martin speaks instead. "Mom, could we get a pizza?"

"I don't know. I was going to start cooking."

"I'd love a pizza," says Beth. "Don't bother to cook." Should she offer to cook? She picks up the afghan strip and smooths it on the table. It is wider than it looks. Reaching out, awkward, from her chair, she hugs Martin from behind with one arm. He doesn't seem to mind.

Franny sounds tired. "Will a large be enough? What kind shall we get? I think two might be too much."

"Onion," says Martin. He goes to consult his brother. They agree on a large meatball-and-onion pizza, and a small mushroom.

"You look tired," says Beth to Jack. Jack looks like someone lost in the lobby of a public building, uncertain whether to find the elevator or explain himself to the deskman. Or is he in the wrong place entirely?

"I'll go," says Franny. She and Beth agree to go together. Franny brings both their coats from the hall closet. She puts her coat down over one of the kitchen chairs and holds Beth's for her. Then she shrugs into her own while Beth is buttoning hers.

Beth's coat is dark brown, new. Alec told her, when she bought it, that he didn't like it. "I know I should. It's a major purchase." He apologizes every time she wears it.

Franny takes a wadded challis scarf out of her pocket and ties it over her head. It is bright red, with a blue paisley design. Beth admires it.

"My ears get cold starting the day after Labor Day," Franny says. This has always been true. Beth and Stephanie can go hatless in any weather. "The baby has your ears," Franny once said on the phone. "She cries if I put a hat on her—and I keep knitting them."

They go out onto the porch. Franny's bike, forgotten, is leaning on its kickstand in front of the house.

"Look at that—it could have been stolen," Franny says.

"Oh, I'm sorry, it's my fault. I forgot all about it when Alec called."

"Philip should have taken care of it."

Franny has pulled the door locked behind them. She rummages in her purse, finds her keys, and opens the door again. It is a tiny house; the door opens into a little foyer and the other rooms are just beyond. She sticks her head in. "Hey, you guys! Would you mind putting my bike away, so we can get going?"

Beth can hear an answering voice. Franny pulls the door closed again. They go down the porch steps and past the bike. As she starts to walk, Beth feels stiff and bruised. Did someone hit her? She remembers her fall.

Franny's car is parked just down the street. It is unlocked. Beth gets into the passenger seat and fastens her seat belt. Franny gets into the driver's seat. She starts the engine and guns it a little, warming up the car. "Jack says I don't need to do this, but I always do. It's like telling the car I'm going to drive it. It makes me feel that it will behave. You know, I'm sorry you came all this way and now you can't see Steffie."

"If this is what she needs, it's OK," Beth says. She sounds insincere to herself.

They pull slowly out of the parking space and up the street, heading back past the house. "I should feel that way, but I can't," Franny says.

It is a narrow street, but parking is permitted on both sides. It is crowded. The small houses here, with their deep porches, are close to one another, with alleys between—no driveways or garages. As they repass Franny and Jack's house, Beth looks out the window on her side.

Martin and Philip have come out in their shirtsleeves. They have put on a light over the basement door, on the side of the house. They have pulled open the slanted cellar doors. Philip is standing halfway down the steep cellar steps, the open doors level with his waist, his arms up, waiting for the bike. Martin is at the top of the stairs, guiding the bike from behind. He has just let the handlebars go, and is leaning over, under the yellow light. His hands are open to catch the seat and the back wheel as they come along, so the bike will not hurtle too quickly down to his waiting brother.

. . . .

A Date with Dmitri

"No. . . . Well, no, actually, I didn't find out what the doctor thinks. I missed the appointment. . . . Can I call you back? There's a sick puppy in New Jersey—" Aunt Mag hangs up. The telephone sits on a small table in the hall. She clicks past me in open-toed shoes and goes back to stirring hard-boiled egg and chicken broth into pungent brown dry dog food. The day is hot. She is in a red-, white-, and black-print sleeveless dress. Her skin is red from working at the stove. She is starting to get fat but her body is still efficient. Her hair is professionally waved, the curl over her left temple elegantly gray, the rest black.

"Your Aunt Mag has done it again," she says. "That was your mother."

I am sitting in the corner of the kitchen, sideways to the gray Formica table, running my finger in the aluminum ridges along its sides. I look at her past a cabinet filled with ceramic pots of undisciplined ivy, detective novels, mail, dusty salt shakers. I lean my head back against the tiled wall. "What did you do?"

"I missed a doctor's appointment. Your mother worked hard to get me to make it. I would have gone, but I had a date with Dmitri."

"Who's Dmitri?"

"Didn't they ever give you that story? I can't remember who wrote it. You'd know, because of being an English major. The one about the dinner party where they're all in some secret revolutionary movement? It must be Russia or someplace. Each guest is trying to imply that in fact *he's* at the center of the action. But the main thing—"

The phone rings. It's not the puppy from New Jersey; it's someone who might buy a dog.

"It's not my bitch," my aunt says. "I'm just passing the information on for a friend. She's a good animal—"

When she gets off the phone, she's talking about the bitch. I remind her about Dmitri.

"Oh—yes—well, what really matters is how well they claim to know this man Dmitri, who's obviously the big shot. One of them has *seen* him in a café. Then another one says he knows where Dmitri lives, but he isn't supposed to say." She puts down a basin of food. Several dogs shoulder into the room to get near it.

"Anyway, there's one country bumpkin. The greenhorn. He just came from the provinces, he doesn't know anything, et cetera, et cetera. Then the bumpkin gets up to leave. They all tease him about being out past his bedtime. Then, of course, wouldn't you know, it turns out he's going to meet Dmitri. Now do you remember it? Who wrote it?"

"No, I never heard of it." I never can remember her stories. It is as if she lives with a private body of literature. "Do the rest of them find out?"

"I can't remember. I wish I could remember who wrote it. I must have read it in high school."

The phone rings. It's the puppy. The puppy is better. My aunt suggests a nutritional supplement.

"Little guy's going to make it. Remember Quiltie?" She is on her way back to the stove.

"No."

"That wasn't her real name. Her real name was Applebaum. Not her registered name, of course. Anyway, she's the mother, Quiltie, Goose's puppy."

"Oh, Goose's puppy." Everyone in this family has at least one nickname. Sometimes the nickname derives from still another nickname. Mag's real name is Sylvia, which itself, according to legend, was Sadie in her youth and possibly something else, something that could be spelled only in Yiddish, before that. I've heard, over the years, several stories about how she came to be Mag.

"That was the litter we named after Steve's professors—they were born the day he graduated. I think Applebaum was sociology."

"But who's Dmitri—you had a date with Dmitri?"

"Oh. Dmitri. A potential stud to mate the Prima Donna with. I mean, the dog's owner. A woman. Rich, influential, owns champions. Everybody tries to get her business. Elizabeth, I think your Aunt Mag has been corrupted by success."

In my family there are no nicknames. I have always wanted one, and have never understood how as an Elizabeth I never managed to become Liz, much less Betty or Beth. For one odd month at girl-scout camp I claimed to be Betsy, but it didn't stick.

The dogs, who are German shepherds, have kennels in the

basement, but spend most of their time in the apartment. Whenever I ring the doorbell they start to bark. Then I hear my aunt's voice—high-pitched, ironic, musical—teasing them by name and nickname into quiet. I see her through the glass pane in the door, coming toward me, hurrying. It must have been a one-family house originally; now it is divided into two apartments, and the renovation has given an odd shape to the first-floor apartment, where my aunt and uncle live. It's bisected by a long narrow corridor with a crowded little foyer at the back, where the phone is. The kitchen is to the left and the living room is beyond it, around toward the front of the house, but nobody seems to enter it except to feed the fish. The bedrooms are off to the right.

The dogs' backs fill the corridor, heaving and shifting like a school of dolphins, with my aunt picking her way through, zigzagging. She opens the door, starting to talk. She is always busy but always pleased to see me and never surprised—or curious about why I might have come. If I do have an errand, I may never get a chance to mention it.

As soon as the door opens, which is difficult, since it opens inward, I am in mid-dog. There are usually five or six of them, all barking. They don't jump or bite. My legs and hips are supported, massaged, pressed on all sides by their bodies, their muscle-backed, short, brushed, black fur. They have big shoulders and heavy tails. Their solid skulls ram my forearms with joy. Bright tan fur outlines their faces, seeming like the light of intelligence. Talking, usually getting back to the phone, Aunt Mag wades toward the kitchen. I make slow progress behind her, greeting dogs.

If it is one of his days off, my uncle may be sitting at the table. He looks up, his mild eyes quiet, with lots of white showing around the brown, not like the dogs' busy, all-dark eyes. My uncle asks questions. If I've been away, he wants to know how my trip was. Was the weather good? And are my parents feeling well?

"I could be lying in the hospital before my sister would think to call," my mother says. "She'd be too busy saving some puppy."

"It would be more complicated than that," I protest, relishing my words. "The puppy would be up in a tree, and the owner of the ladder to rescue the puppy would be at his daughter's wedding—then the groom wouldn't have any pants on, and the man who rented out wedding suits would be demanding to be paid in advance, in puppies."

"Oh, you know me," Aunt Mag tells me on her way from the phone. "We missed the plane. First the luncheon for the priest—don't *ask* how your Jewish aunt got invited to the ordination of a Catholic priest—then Gabby borrowed the car, which I know I swore would never happen again, but I let her do it because Nick was going with her. Well, wouldn't you know it, no sooner did they get to the golf course—"

"Why did they go to the golf course?"

"The pro is a member of the dog club, didn't I tell you? He bought one of Birdie's puppies three years ago. He had the minutes to be typed. I promised I'd type them if they'd make somebody else take notes—that's really why I lent Gabby the car, because she said she'd get them, but then Nick turned his ankle—"

Gabby, the Bathrobe Shakespeare, lives upstairs. She is a single woman in her thirties. Sometimes she works for her father, a doctor, filling in for his regular receptionist; or she goes in on a Sunday and does his books. Mostly she stays home in her bathrobe and writes plays. It is a pink chenille robe, the kind without buttons, held closed by a knotted belt. It clashes with her orange hair, which sticks out from her head in short, straight thickets. She wanders when she writes, and often I find her leaning into Aunt Mag's kitchen from the foyer, always as if she is about to go, always with an empty cup—but no saucer—in her hand. She fixes herself coffee and carries it down, drinks it standing, talking and listening to my aunt, her landlady, and then dangles it from her finger, sometimes twirling it. She nearly drains the cup, but not quite, so the bathrobe has tiny rows of spatter marks here and there.

Sometimes Gabby brings her typewriter down and works in my aunt's kitchen. At first there is a reason—I think the very first time it is because workmen are fixing her sink, though surely no plumber is more distracting than Aunt Mag. Eventually, though, Gabby makes it her habit to write downstairs. I am jealous of her, partly because she always forgets who I am. We are constantly being introduced by Aunt Mag. "I think we've met," I say. Also, with Gabby around it is even less possible to talk to my aunt, though Gabby insists she can't hear us when she is working.

I have taken a creative-writing course myself by this time, and at first would be willing to think of Gabby as a colleague, though all I have written since the course in freshman year are a poem and the beginning of an experimental drama. It doesn't occur to Gabby to offer friendship, though, despite my aunt's frequent references to my being an English major.

One day I try to start a conversation with her about Brecht, but she has never read him. "I get him mixed up with Ibsen," she says. "Those Europeans all remind me of one another."

Aunt Mag seems unconscious of the enormity of this confusion. "I never can remember names either," she puts in. "I forgot the name of the woman who does my hair. You wouldn't think that's possible, because it turns out to be Gertrude, which is the same as the woman who *used* to do my hair. I didn't want her to know I'd forgotten, so I had to call the beauty parlor on her day off and pretend to be somebody else. I asked for Joan, knowing there wasn't a Joan, and I made them reel off the whole list—"

Gabby doesn't seem to get much work done, but eventually a play of hers is produced. Aunt Mag is given two tickets and invites me along. I am sure the play will be terrible, but I accept. My mother has made some remarks about Mag having time for bad plays by strangers when she doesn't seem to have time to look after herself, so I feel that I must go—to defend the life of the spirit. "She may be a great artist," I claim, implausibly.

We take the subway to lower Manhattan. Aunt Mag is dressed up, in a lightweight suit, a hat, and black-and-white high-heeled shoes. It is a summer evening, about six o'clock, and the streets, in this neighborhood of wholesalers whose windows hold displays of Christmas ornaments and "novelties," are empty and shady. It takes us a while to find the building, which looks locked but turns out to be open. We climb to the second floor. To the right is a door with frosted glass and a chipped gold inscription announcing that eyeglasses are made there. The theater is the room on the left, large and stuffy, with a small platform at one end and a clutter of folding chairs.

The room is empty. Finally a man arrives with a young child; then come two young women in shorts.

"If each author got two tickets, this may be the whole crowd," I whisper to Aunt Mag. We have learned from mimeographed programs piled on a chair that there will be three one-act plays.

There are finally about fifteen people. "You'd think there would be more," Aunt Mag whispers as the plays begin. "How often do people have a chance to go to the theater? The last time I saw a play was when that oboist who bought the puppy was in that musical on Broadway, you know—"

The plays are very bad. I am hot. I cannot imagine why I came. Gabby's play is last, and perhaps the worst. About five minutes before it ends, one of the young women in shorts runs out of the room. In a moment we all hear the sound of retching. The actor who is speaking stops and listens, half in character. He seems to be considering working the incident into the play, but decides not to. Aunt Mag, though, slips out, her high heels tapping softly. In a few minutes we hear footsteps on the stairs. She comes back just before the end of the play. During the applause she whispers, "Poor thing couldn't find a bathroom. She's the blond girl's roommate, the one who played the madam in the first play. She says she knew she has that bug that's going around, but she just couldn't disappoint her friend."

"Did somebody clean it up?"

"The roommate came out. She knew where the john was. She brought paper towels. Wouldn't you know it, I actually get to the theater, and somebody throws up."

Gabby comes over to us. For a moment I think she is wearing the bathrobe, but then I see it is a short-sleeved dress of a similar pink. It must be what she wears when she works in her father's office. I imagine hopefully that she will be swept off to a cast party, but she brushes aside the only invitation she gets—a halfhearted one, from the actress whose roommate is sick—and turns to us, clapping a hand on Aunt Mag's shoulder.

"I *love* the end, Gabby—" Aunt Mag begins.

"I'm so depressed," says Gabby. "Can we go somewhere?"

"Of course!" says Aunt Mag. "A celebration." She leads us out through the corridor with the odor of sickness about it, and into the street, where it is still light: it hasn't even gotten dark for Gabby's play. We stand back a bit to let the author of one of the other plays, a boy who looks eighteen, rush past us and down the street alone.

We go to an ice-cream parlor, where Aunt Mag treats Gabby and me to sodas. I claim I am trying to lose weight and insist for a while on coffee, but then I give in. I don't say anything to Gabby about the play.

"Look," Gabby says finally, "I wrote this play four years ago. The woman in charge of the theater chose it from six plays I showed her because—you know why?—because it has three characters. She wanted to call the evening 'One, Two, Three.' So my piece has to follow that nonsense about the dead soldier. Did you get it that he's *already dead*? She *imagines* the whole thing.

"I'm not speaking to any of those people," she goes on. "The director cut a crucial speech—the key to the daughter's character. Then I wanted them to be stuffing a turkey but of course that was too expensive. I could understand that, actually."

"Gabby," says Aunt Mag, "you never know what will come of it."

"Right. That four-year-old might be the drama critic of *The Village Voice*." Noisily, she sucks the last bubbles of her soda up the straw.

"But Gabby," says Aunt Mag, "you're *good*. You're going to make it because you're *good*." I am appalled. I cannot speak. I try to change the subject but Gabby keeps bringing it back.

"You're sure?" she says. "You're sure I'm good?"

We are not alone for a long time, but at last Gabby leaves. She has to go back to the theater, she says. She has some scores to settle.

"Aunt Mag," I say, as we move off together toward the

subway, "Gabby's *terrible.* Can't you tell that?"

She is quiet for a long time. Then, "I know," she says.

My aunt grows fatter, her voice more cheerful, but faster. Her doctor, a gruff man who is rude to everyone and who my mother insists is involved in several criminal conspiracies, becomes harder to avoid. He comes to her house unasked when the entire medical profession has given up house calls. He follows her into the kitchen, scolding her for omitting her pills, for eating too much, staying up late, skipping a test he's ordered.

"You should be lying down right now. You have no business standing over a hot stove in this heat."

"You're right, and I'm going to do it, as soon as I get this dog fed, but you know Bella—it'll be worse if she goes off again and I have to drive her miles to the vet—just stir this, will you?"

"Well," she says to me one day, "it was 'into my cot before light, dear mother' again."

"Dear who?"

"Mother. Don't you remember that one? I thought everyone knew that one—about the girl who stays up dancing every night, and each morning her mother says, 'Did you need the sun to find your bed, my daughter?' meaning, was she up until morning, and the daughter says, no, she was into the cot before dawn, and the whole village scorns her, but then there's an all-night spinning contest or something, and everybody else drops off but she stays awake."

"Does she win and marry the prince?"

"No, she falls asleep just before dawn, the way she always does, so he stays a bachelor. But I think she gets a scholarship to spinning school, or something."

The phone rings. She talks, then goes back to her story—
her own story. She was up until three, working. She's a night
person. It's hard for people to understand this. Her children,
for example, cannot understand it—but she usually sleeps late,
and if she doesn't, surely she doesn't *need* the sleep. And she's
doing well. Another of her dogs has just won Best in Show.
She shows me a photograph. I know the dog, but in the crowded
apartment I've never seen the dignified stance, the effortless
glamour.

She plays with time. Her clock is set ten minutes fast—originally to speed her up in the morning when the children started
school. Now, twenty years later, everyone always, automatically, subtracts ten minutes from her clock, so it can never be
corrected. My parents find this ridiculous, as they found it ridiculous, years ago, when my aunt was so entranced with a
raisin pie she baked on Thanksgiving Day that she and her
family ate it immediately, before dinner—a scene that glittered
in my mind with the glint sometimes of freedom, sometimes,
alarmingly, of disorder.

Her stories become, more often, stories about her sicknesses,
though with the same lilt, the same cadence—"so I got my
friend Jerry to call the doctor. Jerry's a very ipsy-pipsy Park
Avenue surgeon so we thought maybe he'd have a little *in*. And
the doctor, wouldn't you know it, had just been called to explain some germ to the U.N. or the World Health Organization
or something—that's the kind of specialist they bring in for
your aunt, I'll have you know. Well, meanwhile, I blacked out
twice, so I was trying to get more rest, but you know—well,
the upshot was, with the doctor away, nobody could explain
the test until it was too late to start the medicine. Wouldn't
you know it? So now here I am with *double* the dosage and it
still doesn't make any difference.

"And the doctor—not the other doctor, my nice Chinese doctor who's going to give me a recipe for won ton—you know, it's just *kreplach,* but I've never made *kreplach*—well, the doctor says he's never seen it take so long. My luck."

Her legs and ankles swell up. She gets a disease I've never heard of, that covers her body with hideous, painful boils. Then she begins to have trouble breathing.

By now I have moved out of the city, and hear mostly from my mother about how Aunt Mag is doing. My mother still argues with her, when she can get through the busy signals.

"Did you know we talked for half an hour yesterday and she never got off the subject of dogs?" she says. "I finally interrupted her and *demanded* that she tell me how she is, but—"

One summer night my mother calls me, knowing I am going to be in the city the next day. "I cannot persuade my crazy sister not to do this. She's been in bed all week. Now she's got this idea that she has to go look at a litter of puppies that's dying off."

"Why?"

"The vet asked her as a favor—she really is an expert on dog nutrition, I guess. Her claim is that the owner of the puppies is going to pick her up at her door and drive her straight to the animal hospital, get her to look at the puppies, and drive her straight back. Elizabeth, it's so hot. I'm actually afraid she can't make it. Could you possibly go with her?"

"Of course." I call Aunt Mag to tell her I'm "going along for the ride."

"Your mother wants you on the spot, I suppose," she says, "to phone the undertaker."

I take the subway and then the elevated train to her house in Brooklyn the next day. The dogs still fill the corridor, but it

is my uncle who lets me in. "Mag's in bed." But she isn't—
she's pulling on her stockings. She looks heavy and pale but
talks while we wait for the owner, mostly about the puppies.

"Two of them have died. I can't stand it. They're beautiful
animals—well, you'll see."

"Why can't you prescribe over the phone?"

"Oh, no, nothing but a personal consultation will do. Dragged
out of my sickbed. That's the reputation of your old Aunt Mag."

The doorbell rings. The owner of the puppies is a small,
balding man in his fifties, with a sad face. He wrings his hands—
to be precise, he dries them; he pats them together with a
gesture far short of applause. He leads us out, apologizing,
clapping, to his station wagon. We all sit in front. The animal
hospital is in Queens, on a boulevard whose location is vague
to me.

"The grandchildren," mourns the man, whose name is Mr.
Davies. "Mostly it's only my wife and me who fall in love with
the puppies." He cannot pat his hands together when he drives,
but he pats them against the wheel. "This time the grandkids
came for a week, when they started their school vacation, you
know, and now they're in love too." He stops and shakes his
head. "I couldn't tell them that another one died."

Deep in Queens, after Mr. Davies has told us several sad
stories, the car sputters and stops. We are on a long sunny
block, half city street, half highway, with a parking lot next to
us and four lanes of cars going by. Mr. Davies is horrified. He
moves more slowly than ever, but can go back to patting his
hands.

"Mrs. Kaplan," he says, staring under the hood, as we stand
on the pavement watching, "I had no idea—I can't tell you
how upset—"

"Oh, I'm all right," Aunt Mag says cheerfully. "Look, my

niece and I will go get a cab at that corner. You try to flag somebody down, but when we get to the animal hospital we'll call the Triple A. They'll start your car. You meet us there."

It is hot. Aunt Mag and I set out for the corner, the sun reflecting in visible waves off the neatly scored Queens sidewalk, the tiny ailanthus trees in their round beds making feathery pointless shade every twenty yards or so. I can see that the corner up ahead is the beginning of a commercial neighborhood, but I'm frightened. I don't know what will happen if a cab doesn't come.

I try to think what my mother would do. I should have left Aunt Mag in Mr. Davies's car and gone back with a cab to get her, but Mr. Davies is helpless, and the car is hot, and it's stopped in a no-parking lane—there's no parking on this boulevard at all—while cars careen ferociously around it. I am unable to decide what a sensible person would have done—I am no help.

Aunt Mag walks more and more slowly. She can no longer speak. Her breath comes in terrifying short gulps, as if she is constantly being startled. I take her arm but cannot support her bulk. She keeps trying to tell me something—it is not a cry for help. It seems like a joke, but I can't make it out.

At last we reach the corner. After a few minutes, a cab approaches. I wave frantically, but a gray-haired man in a suit steps smartly into the street before me and puts his hand on the door handle.

"Oh, please—" I cry out to him. "Please, can't we have this cab? My aunt is so sick—" The man steps back and turns around. "Oh—" he says. "I didn't know." He opens the door of the cab and takes my aunt's elbow. "Which hospital are you going to?"

Aunt Mag settles herself in the back seat, shifting over to make room for me, though I have rushed around through the traffic to get in on the other side. She leans forward, smiling, to thank the man. Her breath comes back. "Ridgeview Veterinary Hospital," she says clearly.

The man has been bending over, smiling a little, one hand on the cab door, the other starting to point toward the driver—as if to say he's going to make sure of everything. Now he continues to smile, automatically, but I see that he cannot imagine what she means, and he changes the gesture to one that simply gives way to us. He closes the door. Aunt Mag explains to the driver where we are going. She sits back heavily and turns to me. She's going to die, I acknowledge to myself—though not today. "There are two different supplements that would probably fix up those pups," she says to me. "I'm trying to decide which one—which would be the very best thing."

New Haven

New Haven, Connecticut, where Eleanor and Patsy live, is thought to be unusually rich in coincidence. Each new acquaintance there, people claim, turns out to be someone you've met or heard about before—but in a different context. Life there keeps coming back around at you from the other direction. Yet though they expect coincidence, people in New Haven are as surprised by it as anyone else, having imagined that their own strangers will be *strangers*. There's a laughing moment of discomfort when the coincidence comes out, as they wonder how much may be known that had seemed unknown—but then they're glad about it; things, it seems to prove, are connected to one another after all.

The altos must march once more around the folding chair that stands for a tree, right behind the sopranos, but this time they must then veer upstage as they sing, while the sopranos stay put—yet Eleanor, the first alto, can't do it. She's a cellist, actually, but she's still mystified when her eye and arm and fingers carry out different tasks while her mind—well, while her mind seems merely to *wait,* like a mother who sits with her lap full of sweatshirts and towels as her children perform acrobatics. Now she can't get the marching right. "It's too easy for you, that's all," says Catherine, the director of the opera. Each time Eleanor tries, her feet slow and she drifts toward the last soprano, instead of leading the altos to the correct spot. She glares at her errant right leg.

"Once more?" Catherine says. The pianist nods and the men's and women's choruses amble good-naturedly back to their original positions. This time Eleanor feels a hand—is it Patsy's?—tap her rear end at the right moment, and she swerves on the beat.

"OK!"

The rehearsal is over. Eleanor comes forward, breathless, throwing her hair off her shoulders, to explain that she must be late for the next one—but there are tears in the director's eyes.

"What's wrong?" asks Eleanor, jolted from shyness by her new success. Though she has often played in public (her cello a comforting heft tipped toward her) and has sung in glee clubs and choirs since childhood (a score held upright before her chest), Eleanor has never before moved around on a stage, thinking about her feet and getting her bottom slapped.

"Oh. Nothing," says Catherine.

Eleanor steps back; clearly she won't ever know what's wrong. For a forgetful moment she looks around for her cello case. Then she looks for Patsy, her new friend. They've fallen into the habit of going to Clark's Dairy together after the rehearsals. The woman in charge of costumes and props has come over, and now she lowers an arm onto the director's shoulder and steers her away, saying, "All right, you." Eleanor can't tell whether she is going to scold Catherine or comfort her.

"Let's take my car," says Patsy. "I'll drive you back to yours later." They zip up their jackets and follow the other chorus members out through the school basement door and up the steps to the street. It's raining a little.

It's the first warm rain, in fact—so early in February that it can't be spring, but it smells like it. There isn't much snow at the moment; lingering patches of it, their edges gray and soft, are being carved away by the rain. Ordinarily Eleanor would be troubled by Catherine's rebuff, but she doesn't think this has to do with her; along with the melting snow, feeling is simply spilling everywhere—and when a familiar edgy tautness takes its place in her throat, as she steps outside, the way it has for the last six weeks each time a distraction has ended, it's more exciting than painful, as if she'd had a glass of wine. This being in love with Peter, she points out to herself, lives in her neck.

"I'm parked on Willow," says Patsy. They walk that way. "So how are you doing these days?"

"Mixed."

Is she going to tell Patsy about Peter? Unlike Eleanor, Patsy has been married. She has a six-year-old son, Gabriel, who goes to this school, where every few years the PTA stages an opera. Eleanor was recruited for the adult chorus (there are also crowds of children) by the mother of one of her cello pupils. Patsy is raking her fingers through her short curly hair, shaking off raindrops. She seems like the sort of woman who's always at ease about men—a subject they haven't yet discussed.

Eleanor and Patsy first saw each other several months ago, at the music school where Eleanor teaches. She'd been practicing alone in a studio one day—alone because a student had canceled a lesson. She'd finished a long, difficult section of a

Bach suite, and was turning the pages back to try it again, when the door opened and a woman's dark curly head appeared. "Thanks," the woman—Patsy—said. "Sorry. I'm just standing out here waiting for my kid. But I had to say thanks." Then, on the night of the first rehearsal of the opera, Patsy came up to her. "You're that *cellist*."

But Eleanor has never even slept with Peter—her old-fashioned rapture may amuse Patsy. They reach the car. Eleanor climbs in and looks out at the rain while Patsy walks around into the street, gets in, and starts the engine and switches on the windshield wipers. How unusual for Eleanor—she's going to tell.

"Mixed?" Patsy asks.

And she does. "I should be feeling wonderful," she says, counting her blessings on her fingers. "I'm happy about the piece I'm learning. My teaching is fine. And there's a violinist who wants me to be in groups he puts together that play at weddings and parties. It should be fun, and I can use the money."

"Terrific."

"It's too terrific. He's—the violinist—married, and I'm sort of in love with him."

"Oh. Oh dear, that's hard." They drive down Whitney Avenue. "Does he know how you feel?"

"Yes." She thinks of the other night, when she and Peter had a drink together, how the conversation seemed finished but kept being reopened, how Peter finally took out some bills to put under the check at the edge of the table, but when he did they'd have to go home, so he smoothed them again and again, then shook them into a congruent pile and folded them crisply in half—no, in thirds.

"Does he feel the same way?" asks Patsy.

"Yes." How could she talk about it if he didn't? "He keeps saying to me," she goes on, " 'I'm not really like this. Please don't think I'm like this.' "

"Oh, dear." As she parks the car on Temple Street, Patsy glances at Eleanor. "Are you sleeping with him?"

"No," says Eleanor, laughing: *that* didn't take long. She's a little ashamed to lack her secret suddenly, but as they get out of the car and walk back toward Trumbull Street and around the place where Temple and Whitney converge—it's raining a little harder now—she also feels pleased; she doesn't have to guard it, for once. And it's exhilarating to talk about Peter.

Clark's is crowded. There is even a crowd at the ice-cream-cone counter, as if it were spring. Patsy and Eleanor work their way to the back of the dairy and find a table.

"Well," says Patsy, "I know how you feel."

"You do?"

"In a way, I do. Well. I should tell you. I've been sleeping with a married man for two years."

They decline menus. Eleanor just wants coffee—she can't eat these days. Patsy orders a dish of ice cream.

"Two years," says Eleanor. Patsy's confidence is more interesting than hers.

"I hate it," says Patsy. "Well, it's wonderful—and I don't mind living without a man. But it doesn't make a woman self-confident."

"No, I imagine not." Eleanor has turned shy again. She should ask a question. She'd like to know the man's name, for some reason, but of course that wouldn't do. "Do you see him often?"

"Sometimes," Patsy says. "Sometimes I pull away, like when I catch myself sneering at his wife. I hate that. I don't even know her."

The coffee and ice cream arrive. Eleanor sips eagerly, hoping the warmth of the coffee will put her at ease again. Thinking it over, she says, "I like the way you talk about it, though." She doesn't know Peter's wife either.

"It isn't good," says Patsy. "It keeps me from thinking about other things. My son. Work. It steals my thoughts. I'm ending it."

Swiftly, Eleanor imagines a two-year affair with Peter—pain, guilt, the end. . . .

"I'm moving away from New Haven," Patsy goes on. "It's the only way. I'm going back to school—I'm going to live in Boston and get an M.S.W. I'm leaving in June when Gabe is done with school."

"I'll miss you."

"Thanks. I'll miss you, too. It'll be hard to leave New Haven, for a lot of reasons."

"How long have you lived here?"

"I was born here," says Patsy. "When I was married we lived in California, but I came back when we split up."

So there will be no friendship after all. Eleanor gropes for a less personal topic, and they talk about Boston. A little while later, though, Patsy interrupts herself. "But you were telling me about this man and I cut you off. I'm sorry. See? I'm getting self-centered."

"It's OK." But she is pleased again.

"You're going through the tough part."

"Mostly, I try to stop loving him," says Eleanor. "But that doesn't work."

"Never has," says Patsy. "Though it's what my mother would say to do—and she's never *entirely* wrong." Her ice cream is gone. The waitress is writing up the check. Walking back to Patsy's car in the rain, which is more like mist now, they talk about mothers.

* * *

Eleanor figures that there are only two ways to stand a wedding. One is the way she and Peter, half a string quartet, fell into the first time they played at one, well over a year ago, on a day they would end by sleeping together for the first time. All day long they *used* the wedding, sending silly, loving, questing signals over the music stands and the heads of the other musicians, allowing themselves, for once, to forget the big questions by pretending to worry about what wasn't in doubt— whether they'd end up in bed.

But that way hasn't worked for a while. The second way to bear a wedding is to dismiss it. For that day, Eleanor is nothing but a musician. She plays for an imaginary chamber-music-loving uncle among the guests. He will drift over, drink in hand, to ask how he can hear her again. Once, something of the sort even happened—it was the groom's old roommate, actually, a pianist from Chicago, and they talked about Beethoven for an hour.

A third possible way to do weddings—the one she cannot stand—is the one she will probably adopt today, she thinks, as she waits for Peter's car in the sun outside her house. It's a humid day in August. She's been told that the wedding as well as the reception will be on the grounds of the bride's parents' house. She's worried about her cello in the damp weather— strings slipping, bad sound. She and Peter are to perform before the ceremony with a flutist whom Eleanor met at the practice session the other day; then, after a break, they will play during dinner. It will be a long day.

"What if it rains?" she'd asked.

"Tents."

The bad way to do weddings—today's way—is to spend them imagining Peter's wedding, three years ago, to the difficult and complicated Abby, with whom he may or may not spend the rest of his life.

And she hasn't even had the sense to put up her hair. Eleanor's hair is long, thick, and straight. It looks good loose, the way she wears it, but the back of her dress is already damp. In this weather, strands of hair will snag and crawl over her face and into her mouth, even her eyes. Playing, she won't be able to flick them out.

Peter's small brown car swings abruptly to the curb. His arm reaches to the back seat behind Rebecca, the flutist, and his hand flips up the lock on the back door. Eleanor maneuvers her cello in first and slides in behind Rebecca.

"Sorry I'm late," says Peter.

"Hi," says Rebecca. "It's my fault for living in Guilford. I should have come by myself."

"I bring *everybody,*" said Peter. "The one time I tried it the other way, sure enough somebody got lost. He kept phoning to say he was *still* lost."

"Well, actually, my husband and I have only one reliable car," says Rebecca. "This way, he can take the kids to the beach. Though he did look wistful, watching me leave on a Sunday. Is that a problem you have too?" She twists her head to look at Eleanor.

"I live alone," says Eleanor, but her words are lost in Peter's answer. Looking ahead, he thinks Rebecca is talking to him. "Sometimes, yes," he is saying. "Sometimes my wife would rather be by herself. Right now, she's out of town for the weekend, visiting a friend."

Eleanor looks out the window. The wedding is in Woodbridge; they are driving out Whalley Avenue. She hadn't known Abby was away. On the wide, hot sidewalk there is nobody but a woman pushing a stroller, with a little girl walking beside her. Peter stops for a red light. The girl is crying—her sneaker has come off. Her mother is bending over, trying to put it back on, keeping one hand on the stroller while the girl tries to keep her bare foot off the burning pavement, balancing herself by holding on to her mother's shoulder. The mother can't get the sneaker over the child's heel; as the light changes and Peter pulls away, she stands up to work the laces open, frowning in concentration, while the child hops and cries. Eleanor wishes she had the nerve to make Peter stop and let her out; trundling her cello, she'd run away from him and go help them. She could hold the stroller. Or *she* could open the laces. She's good with knots.

"Is this a first marriage, with a long white dress?" Rebecca is asking.

"His first, her second," says Peter. "I don't know about the dress, but I think the whole thing will be pretty casual. He's close to forty, I guess. I haven't met her. He's the brother of a neighbor of mine—he moved here about a year ago. There's a story about him, but I forget it."

They drive out Fountain Street toward Woodbridge. "I've been lost around here," says Rebecca.

"I've memorized the directions," says Peter, and he has.

There are two tents. Chairs for the ceremony are arranged outside, in informal clusters. There are fifty guests, Eleanor estimates. The wedding is to be performed by a nervous-looking young rabbi.

She and Peter and Rebecca play Haydn. They are under an open tent, a little to the side of the guests, between the improvised outdoor chapel and the bride's parents' house. The tent is supposed to give them shade, but a ray of sunlight intermittently pokes Eleanor in the eye, depending on how a low-hanging nearby maple bough is jostled by the light breeze. There it is again. Between movements, she shifts her folding chair a little, but now one chair leg tips into a small depression in the ground. As she feels the chair lurch slightly, a corresponding sensation—an obstinate need for Peter, who's nodding briskly to start the next movement—travels through her body. She imagines herself sent sprawling by it, chair down, falling into the dirt with her cello on top of her.

The rabbi is taking his place in front of the guests and a few attendants join him, their informality almost studied; the women, in print dresses, turn to one another as they come forward, chatting a little. The groom, whose name, she has gathered, is Harry, has been talking to a very old man. Now he embraces him hastily and walks arm in arm with another man to the place where the ceremony will be performed. Eleanor knows that at a Jewish wedding the bride and groom walk in with their parents. Perhaps the groom has no mother.

The bride has not appeared, but now a man—her father, it seems—comes out of the house by a side door and down the few steps. Out of the corner of her eye Eleanor can see him standing with his back to the guests, shifting his feet as if he's in a hurry; he might be a man alone in his backyard, waiting for his family so they can leave on an ordinary outing. Now the screen door bangs. Two women have come out. They pause on the steps. Eleanor, with one eye on the music, can see the bride, in a blue dress, put a hand on her mother's shoulder. They walk down the three steps off the porch. The bride swings her arms back and then forward, seizing her parents' hands in a gesture of ease and good cheer.

Her mother is laughing a little, hurrying across the grass in high heels. Halfway to the group awaiting them, just as the father passes in front of Eleanor, the bride turns to him, as if to whisper a wisecrack. Eleanor, looking up over her bowing arm, sees the bride's face: it's Patsy.

But that can't be the married lover, can it? Eleanor asks herself later, as Patsy and Harry make their way from guest to guest. Patsy doesn't seem to have noticed her yet. She and Peter and Rebecca are free until dinnertime. The two other musicians have wandered off, but Eleanor is sitting on a bench, leaning back against the picnic table—her cello is in its case in the shade—watching the guests. Two waiters with trays move among them across the lawn, in and out of swatches of sunlight, offering glasses of champagne.

No—of course it's a different man, if Peter is correct that Harry has only recently moved to New Haven and has never been married before. She last saw Patsy at the cast party after the opera, over a year ago, just before the move to Boston. They'd hugged each other good-bye—but then Eleanor put that friendship out of her mind. She'd wanted it rather badly.

She's hotter than ever. She wishes they didn't have to play through dinner. It would be good to be alone; she knows Peter won't arrange anything for tonight, though a part of her mind can't quite drop the idea.

She goes over to the bar that's been set up in the other tent and asks for plain club soda. The bartender puts a wedge of lemon in. Eleanor returns to her bench. Sipping, she watches the guests, trying to play the game she plays at weddings when she's feeling good: that woman must be the bride's aunt—she's clearly the mother's sister—but who's the child?

Patsy, she sees, has turned away from her husband. She comes across the lawn, conspicuous in her light-blue full-skirted dress,

stepping quickly, then stopping to laugh and accept congratulations. Now she hurries into the tent and Eleanor is seized
in a silky, sweaty hug.

"I can't believe this," says Patsy.

"Hey, congratulations. Good luck."

"I couldn't believe it when I came out of the house and saw
you. I've missed you. And there are very few people here from
New Haven. Most of my friends are floating rafts down the
Colorado River. Never get married in August."

"Well, it's me," says Eleanor.

"I have to talk to you." Patsy sits down on the bench. "Eleanor,
I have to ask you. Is that *him*?"

"What?"

"Him. The violinist. The man you told me about."

She'd thought Patsy wouldn't remember. She turns and looks
at the bride.

"I think it is," says Patsy, "and it's still going on, and it's
driving you crazy, and you have to sit and play at *weddings,* of
all things, trying to guess what's in his head. I've been thinking
that since I saw you here."

So Eleanor puts her glass of soda down on the table and
cries. She lets Patsy stroke her hand. Peter and Rebecca, over
near the side of the house, are watching her. Peter looks angry,
but she doesn't care.

Patsy waits.

"But Patsy," she finally says, swallowing some more soda to
quiet herself. "This man—your husband—he isn't—"

"Oh, no. I couldn't believe it when I recognized you," says
Patsy. "You're the only person here who knows about Keith.
Really knows. Harry sort of knows. I hope you're going to *like*
Harry."

"Of course I will," says Eleanor.

"I met him the week before I moved," says Patsy. "I've spent the entire year in my car driving up or down between here and Boston, dragging Gabriel. At least he and Harry get along. We're moving back here. I really can't live anywhere but New Haven." She looks around at the graceful tree-bordered yard.

"But I liked Boston," she continues, "and I finished my course work. I have a field placement here. Of course, I'm a little nervous about living in the same city as Keith again. That's his name, the man I told you about that night—Keith. But I'm very happy and I think I know what I'm doing."

Eleanor has stopped crying. She looks out of the tent at the healthy green lawn, and into the surrounding bit of woods; it's dense enough to seem dark and cool. At the edge are low bushes, but Eleanor can see an open place where someone could walk in under the trees.

Peter has come over to them. "The caterer tells me dinner is in fifteen minutes," he says to Eleanor. "We play again—OK?"

She introduces him to Patsy. They shake hands.

"At least they're keeping to their schedule," he says to Eleanor. "I've got to get home at a reasonable hour—I still have all those papers to grade." He turns to Patsy. "I'm teaching history of music in summer school," he explains. "Grades are due tomorrow." He walks away again.

"Oh boy," says Patsy, laughing.

Eleanor laughs too. "Oh, Patsy," she says. "Welcome home. I need you. I'm a mess. For one thing, I'm so hot I'm going to die."

"I know. This dress feels like it's made of rubber," says Patsy. "And you with that hair—" She rotates Eleanor away from her and lifts her hair with both hands. Eleanor feels the air touch her neck. "Though you do have great hair." Patsy combs Eleanor's hair with her fingers, gathering in each loose strand. Eleanor feels a firm tug as it is all swept off her neck.

"I'm braiding it for you," Patsy says. She has been dividing Eleanor's hair into three sections. Now the slight tugging moves back and forth from one side of Eleanor's head to the other as Patsy forms the sections into a long braid. Eleanor waits quietly until Patsy comes to the end—lightened, surprised to be letting herself be helped.

Patsy says, "I don't suppose you have anything to fasten this with?"

"No."

"Wait a minute. My mother's junk drawer. Ponytail holders." She hands Eleanor the end of the braid and walks quickly toward the house.

The braid is so long that Eleanor can hold it easily. She brushes the tip against her cheek. It feels like an animal's tail. She waits, looking out at the tiny woods. Soon she sees Patsy coming toward her again, displaying in her hand a ponytail holder—the kind made of glittery elastic fastened into a circle with a bit of gold-colored metal. Patsy holds it up between thumb and forefinger, a little O—just what she wanted, just what she knew she'd find in the drawer.

. . . .

In Family

Stephanie, who is ten, would like to know exactly how old her great-grandmother is—ninety-five or ninety-six? Jack, Stephanie's father, doesn't know.

"But didn't you know when you were a little boy? Didn't you go to her birthday parties?"

He tells her he doesn't think his grandmother, who grew up in Russia, celebrates birthdays.

"But when they got a new president in Russia, I remember they said on television how old *he* was."

This sounds plausible, but Jack cannot satisfy her. He feels bad about discussing his grandmother, because they are in the same room with her, here in her nursing home, but it is easier to have a conversation with Stephanie than with Grandma. The old woman is in a wheelchair. Her feet, in heavy socks, are motionless on the footrests, and her knees are apart, with her blue plaid cotton housedress wrinkled over them. Her white hair, which was always in a bun, is now cut short; it is thin and stands away from her head. She looks with interest from father to daughter. Jack doesn't know how clear her mind is— whether she can follow the conversation.

"I was born in Russia," she says with dignity. Her voice is shaky but its accent is still familiar to Jack, who believed as a child that speaking with a foreign accent was an unvarying characteristic of grandparents. "And my husband, and also my son Abe."

"Abe is my father, Grandma," says Jack. "I'm Jack."

"He has beautiful children," says his grandmother. She is speaking of Jack himself. "Three children. The girl is Steffie."

"Steffie is *me!*" Stephanie starts to laugh but stops herself.

"Let me look at you," says the grandmother to Stephanie, who moves a few inches nearer the wheelchair and stands with her firm legs together; they are bare below her blue-and-white shorts. She has a round belly that looks bigger than it is be- cause her posture is a little self-conscious. She plays with the white trimming on the hem of the shorts as if she's trying to work it loose. She's a little too large for her gestures. Jack is touched by her awkwardness and reaches out toward her just as his grandmother takes Stephanie's hands and holds them, laughing—an elemental laugh, all open mouth, because her face has so little flesh.

"Daddy, can I push her?" Stephanie means the wheelchair. Jack doesn't know what to say. He doesn't know the rules of the nursing home, or what his grandmother would like. He has never visited his grandmother here without his father com- ing along too; his father, a retired teacher, lives in Brooklyn. Up to now, a visit to the nursing home, which is in Queens, has been part of a long day in New York for Jack, with his whole family in attendance and sometimes his brother's family as well. This time, he and Stephanie have driven down alone from New Haven, where they live, and he didn't even tell his father that they were making the trip.

"Grandma, should we take you to the canteen?" he says now. "Or to the sunroom, maybe?"

Now Jack notices a young man and woman standing in the doorway. He assumes they are looking for his grandmother's roommate, who was on her way out of the room with her walker when they arrived; he remembers a lounge with a television set—perhaps she is there.

"Jack!" says the young man. "It's *years.*" It is his cousin David, coming forward and shaking his hand. "What are you doing here? Did you drive in from New Haven?"

"We took the boat," says Stephanie.

"You can come here from New Haven by *boat?*"

"I'd always wanted to try it," says Jack. He is not sure whether David has seen that he didn't recognize him at first. "It's a car ferry from Bridgeport to Port Jefferson. Stephanie loved it."

"No I didn't," says Stephanie. "I was cold."

"*I* loved it," Jack corrects himself.

"*You* loved it, of course," David says. "You. The old adventurer."

This is not the way Jack thinks of himself. David gestures to show that they've gotten ahead of themselves. "Then this is Steffie," he says.

Jack is trying to remember what he knows about David, who is several years younger than he is. David's mother is Jack's father's youngest sister. Jack and his wife, Franny, attended David's wedding, he remembers now—maybe three years ago, at a motel on Long Island. They had to leave the children with Franny's sister. Franny was angry, because Martin was still nursing; she wanted to take him along. Then it must have been more than three years ago.

"Tanya," Jack says, having remembered David's wife's name.

"Oh. No," says David, laughing a little. "Actually, Tanya and I have been separated for two years. This is my friend Julie."

"Hi," says Julie.

"I'm sorry," says Jack. "I must have known." He wonders whether it is worse if he didn't know or if he forgot. David is kissing their grandmother.

"Grandma, this is Julie," David says. "Remember? We took you out on the town."

"A very sweet girl," says the grandmother.

"The last time we came, we took her for a walk," David says to Jack. "There's sort of a playground. We bought her ice cream."

"Daddy, let's go there," says Stephanie. "When are we going to leave?"

David sits down on the edge of the grandmother's bed. Jack is already sitting in the only chair provided for his grandmother's visitors, a Scandinavian-style armchair with a low wooden back that cuts into his shoulders. Now Julie pulls over the one next to the roommate's bed. They make a cramped group around the wheelchair. Stephanie leans against Jack, half sitting on the arm of his chair.

David reaches over to the wheelchair, takes their grandmother's hand in his, and strokes it rhythmically. He acts as if he were in charge here. Jack feels inert and vague beside him. It would be better if he were more like David. He would come here more often and feel more relaxed afterward. As it is, he hasn't been here to see his grandmother for more than a year now. For some reason, he doesn't have much contact with this part of his family, although he has ten first cousins from this, his father's, side. On his mother's side there are only three, and Jack is in touch with all of them. None of them could marry or divorce without his knowing all about it. One, Janet, is chronically ill. He feels a momentary irritation with David simply for claiming him as a cousin, as if this unfamiliar man, whose profession Jack can't recollect, were the same to him as his difficult, quarrelsome Janet, struggling to teach kindergarten in Boston, never quite well.

"So you're Stephanie," Julie says. "I know all about you. You play the recorder."

Stephanie doesn't answer.

"Grandma," says David, "I got the apartment. I sign the lease tomorrow."

"You have to move?" says the old lady.

"I *want* to. Don't you remember? I told you." Turning to Jack, he says, "She can't imagine that anybody would want to move. She lived in that same place on Bedford Avenue for— what, Grandma, thirty years? Forty?"

He turns to Julie. "I loved going there. Jack, I always hoped you'd play with me at those big family parties, even though you were so much older." He turns to Julie again. Each time he speaks to one of them, David leans forward and his upper body swivels in the appropriate direction, as if they were in such a large room that the person whose attention he wanted might have forgotten to listen. Now he turns to Julie again. "My cousin Jack was the intellectual. Jack, do you remember the time you took the rest of us to Prospect Park and got us lost?"

Jack remembers—he thinks of the fight with his father later that day, and the angry tears. It's been twenty-five years, but this old family story still gives him pain. Nothing happened, really. He remembers the start of that afternoon, when he led his cousins off through Prospect Park as if he knew all its pathways and turnings by heart, and how frightened he had suddenly felt when the expedition went wrong and the other boys first realized that they were lost and that he had been pretending to an ease he didn't possess.

Mostly, though, his memory of visiting his grandmother's apartment is of boredom. He cannot remember playing with anyone. His grandmother didn't seem to enjoy visitors. He has always suspected that she would have preferred to remain single, a solitary working woman—she was a good seamstress. What he liked best about her apartment was the smell of clean, worn cloth. He'd find something to read there and wait for his parents to be ready to go. But how does Julie know that Stephanie plays the recorder—or, more accurately, did for a few months, in an after-school program about a year ago.

"Grandma," says David, "remember the time Jack got us lost in Prospect Park? Me and Michael and Barry—was Barry there? Do you remember the policeman, Jack? And how your father came running up to us?" He turns to Julie, who is listening with pleasure—but so is Grandma. "He kept shouting, 'Officer! Officer! I'm coming!' I think your dad thought we'd all be arrested."

Although Jack does remember the policeman and although he knows that their cousin Barry *wasn't* with them that afternoon, he doesn't answer.

"I'd give anything for memories like that," Julie says.

"Daddy, I'm so cold. I'm going to be so cold on that boat." It's an hour later. Jack and Stephanie have found the playground and an ice-cream vendor; being cold hasn't stopped Stephanie from wanting a Popsicle. It's purple, and Jack finds himself thinking automatically about its artificial color and flavor. Stephanie has a purple stain around her mouth and purple streaks congealing on her legs.

"You know what, Steff," Jack says, "I think we should stop

at a store and buy you a sweater. I'd hate for you to miss being out on deck." She insisted on staying in the enclosed part of the boat this morning; he'd like to see her get excited about this fairly rare trip across water.

"How will we find a store?" Stephanie asks.

"Oh, we'll pass one." Stephanie, her Popsicle finished, goes off to look around, while Jack waits on a bench in the sun. It really is a chilly day, bright and dry but windy. They'd expected it to be warm, and neither of them took along a jacket in the rush to drive to the ferry this morning. The park has a playground crowded with wooden turrets, ladders, and ramps, not just swings and slides. Jack notices that Stephanie's mouth is moving as she walks around a little parapet and up and down a ramp. She must be talking to herself.

Having mentioned the sweater, Jack has become anxious about it. Buying it seems wasteful—surely Stephanie owns enough sweaters, if they'd only thought to bring one along. He points out to himself that the weather may change and Stephanie won't need a sweater. His grandmother, who has always known about clothing, would disapprove of whatever it is he is about to buy. He pictures her, with her hair the old way, fingering a sleeve with distaste.

When he kissed her good-bye in the nursing home, she said, "A nice kiss." For a moment, Jack felt sure that she knew who he was. He is surprised that it matters to him whether she knew, whether she was glad to see him. He would like to be chuckling now over her old crankiness, and, noting that wish in himself, he sees what else he'd like—that he, not David, be the attentive sort of grandson, teasing his grandmother and talking at her, whether she understood him or not, and that Stephanie be the sort of confident child who is at ease anywhere, who is never cold.

It would have been easier for him, he thinks oddly, if some-how he could have visited his other grandmother, his mother's mother, if she had lived on into her nineties like this. His mind goes back to one of the few times he ever saw his two grand-mothers together—the morning before his high-school gradu-ation, when they had both come to his parents' house, *his* house, where the family was getting ready to leave for the ceremony. But when Jack put on his rented cap and gown so they could take pictures, it was discovered that the hem of the gown was uneven, dipping wildly at one side. His father's mother—this grandmother—asked for needle and thread (and a thimble, which Jack's mother didn't have). She made Jack stand on a chair he brought from the kitchen and set about ripping out and sewing several inches of the hem, kneeling on the rug. His other grandmother watched from a chair. Then she went into the kitchen and returned with a piece of bread.

"Eat." She handed it to Jack.

"Why?" Jack didn't know what she wanted, but he began nibbling the bread.

"Better to eat while your grandma fixes. Nothing bad should happen." She sat down and watched again.

"My mother also," said the sewing grandmother from the floor after a pause, her voice a little scornful of Jack's other, more old-fashioned grandmother—teaching a superstition to a child!—"my mother would give me to eat, if she needed to fix while I was wearing."

It must have felt strange to him to see them together. He stood there as the hemming went on, rotating slowly in his gown like a mechanical graduating boy on a cake, and obedi-ently chewing on the piece of rye bread. In the memory, the grandmothers waft toward him from their two directions like different kinds of music or different smells: one woman (now long dead) ceremonial, loving, and foolish, happy to be a grandmother, the other—the survivor—impatient, clever, restless in her generation, restless in family. He tries to explain to himself that the woman he has just seen is the same person who knelt on the rug.

But they should start—the last ferry to Connecticut is at six. He calls to Stephanie, and they walk back to their car.

It takes longer than he expects to find a store where they can buy a sweater. Finally he stops at a gas station, and they are directed to a shopping center half a mile or so off their route. Stephanie is excited, and when there are no sweaters in stock for girls her size, she cheerfully selects a pink nylon jacket with a zipper up the front. It has absurd white cotton lace on the neck and wrists. Jack thinks she would look better in a plain blue one but she says that the one he likes is a boy's jacket.

They have to wait on line for a long time to pay for the jacket, and when they have left the store and made their way out of the parking lot it takes a while to get back on their route. Then, on the parkway, they find themselves caught in heavy traffic. Stephanie is in the back seat, the jacket in a plastic drawstring sack in her lap. She falls asleep. Jack becomes afraid they will miss the ferry. He is beginning to feel stupid. There will be no pleasure in telling the story of missing the ferry on himself. It was a mistake to buy the jacket; stopping for it will have made them late.

If they miss the ferry they'll have to turn around and drive all the way back through Long Island, back into Queens, across the Throgs Neck Bridge, and then to New Haven along the Connecticut Turnpike—an enormous journey. They are moving steadily now, but slowly. There is a slight rise, and when they reach the top he can see that the cars in both lanes going in his direction are stopped a quarter of a mile away—there is a long line of them with brake lights on. He looks at the farthest car he can see and wills it to be released and move.

Stephanie wakes up. "I'm thirsty," she says.

"We'll get a drink on the boat."

"Can't we stop now and get a drink?"

"Steffie, *no*—-I'm afraid we're going to miss the boat as it is."

"Well, if we miss it can we stop and get a drink *after* we miss it?"

He laughs, but then he says, "Steff, I'm nervous, and if you make me talk I'll get mad."

They reach the ferry on time. They drive their car up the metal clanking ramps and then down to park it in the garage section. They climb out and head up to the deck. There is a stiff wind blowing. Stephanie takes her jacket out of its plastic bag and makes her father remove the tags. She sees a trash basket over by the deckhouse and runs to throw the tags into it but asks him to hold the bag, which she wants to keep. On the way back to him, she slips on a wet spot on the deck and falls. Jack runs toward her but she jumps up again, impatient with his concern. Fighting the wind, she puts the jacket on and zips it closed. Then she takes back the plastic sack and stuffs it into the pocket. She and Jack walk to the rail and lean over. The engines start up underneath their feet and then there is dark water between the boat and the dock. They watch it grow wider. When they turn and stroll down the deck, they are caught by the wind, which makes Stephanie's pink jacket billow up like a little sail. Jack sees that the jacket is long on her; it comes below her shorts and could be all she has on, besides her sneakers. Jack likes the look of her, even the purple streaks from the Popsicle. She reminds him of someone in a costume—a court jester, perhaps, someone bravely jaunty. There is one more tag they hadn't noticed flapping behind her.

Stephanie says, "Do you think Great-Grandma gets embarrassed when she says things wrong?" She has to shout to be heard over the sound of the engines and the wind.

"I don't know!" he shouts back. "I THINK—MAYBE—NOT."

"When I'm in my nineties I'm not going to say anything—just to make sure," Stephanie says loudly. She spreads her arms. "I'm blowing away!" She runs from Jack to the railing on the opposite side of the deck and then full tilt—almost full tilt—straight at him, and throws herself against him. Her hair feels soft and tangled on his chest but her head is hard. He knows he's not supposed to put his arm around her—it's a game. Sure enough, she is bouncing off him to run back across the deck. Then again she runs into him. She is pretending to be helpless in the wind and under the force of her own energy, but he can tell by the feel of her landing that she isn't. There's just a little control at the last second, a little restraint. How many of us, he asks himself, can just let go?

Exactments

People who grew up without relatives idealize them, but I spent my childhood surrounded by aunts and uncles, and I usually think of them—this is a terrible thing to say—as irritating, stupid people. They offer love, all right, but a love intended for someone subtly different from me. When I was a child, my Aunt Ruthie and Aunt Sylvie—my mother's sisters—and Aunt Sylvie's husband, Uncle Mike, came to dinner every Sunday. I'd admired Aunt Ruthie, the youngest of the three sisters, when I was little, but she had gradually become younger even than I was, somehow, and when I was eleven or so I was often taken aback by things she'd say, though if I tried to define later what it was about Ruthie, my mother insisted she didn't know what I was talking about.

"There's nothing wrong with Ruthie," she said. "You're a snob about her. She never had your opportunities."

"That's not what I mean," I said.

Aunt Ruthie and I both collected picture postcards. I kept mine in a shoe box. Once a chain letter came in the mail, saying that if I sent a picture postcard to the first of four strangers on a list, and a copy of the letter to ten people I knew, in a few days I'd have hundreds of postcards. I spent hours copying the letter, though my father said I was asking to be heartbroken. Weeks later, I received a single postcard, from a girl in Chicago—an outcome, by the way, that satisfied me. It seemed to prove my father wrong.

Aunt Ruthie, of course, had been one of my ten people. She was hurt when the chain letter didn't work, though she got two cards, one from New Jersey and one from Albany. I couldn't persuade her not to feel bad about it. "Still nothing special in the mail," she said, for weeks.

Ruthie always insisted that postcards didn't count unless they had been sent, which probably led to my loss of interest in collecting them, because I thought she might be right and my whole collection didn't quite count, that it was only a "sort of" collection. But it was too hard to wait for people to send them. By the time I was a teenager, I'd forgotten about postcards, and was annoyed when Aunt Ruthie followed me into my bedroom, wanting to look over the pile again. Sometimes I pretended I didn't know where the shoe box was.

Aunt Ruthie is still collecting picture postcards, I discovered recently, and she still thinks I might be. I'm a doctor—I've just finished a residency in pediatrics. I shouldn't be angry that Ruthie doesn't know what a residency is, even after I've explained it. I have had all the luck, and Ruthie has had none. She's a file clerk. She lives alone, and spends all her time with my other aunt, who's passive-aggressive—my mother says that's not true either—and my uncle, who's just boring. When I am with her—with all of them—I'm not sure I haven't turned back into the girl they seem to think I am. On the other hand, I don't want them ever to die.

On a Saturday morning last March I was awakened by the sound of my brother Jeffrey's front door being pulled shut as slowly as possible. I was sleeping on his sofa. He was going running, trying to leave quietly, but the door was near my head and I woke up anyway. I listened to the sound of the lock snapping, and then Jeffrey's key turning over the mechanism in the second lock. I was touched, as if he were being unusually kind, and then I identified my feeling: several weeks earlier, the man I'd been living with had broken up with me and moved out, and I'd been feeling bad—but now I'd entered a second, convalescent stage, when any gesture that isn't actually hostile feels like the touch of a healer. I lay there quietly until Jeffrey came back and tiptoed past me, and I didn't get up until after I'd heard the shower, when he started making noises in the kitchen.

I was in New York for an interview with a pediatrics practice—I'd flown in from Michigan, where I did my residency, on Thursday, and the interview had been on Friday. I was staying with Jeffrey because my parents, who are retired, were away, on a trip to Mexico looking at pyramids. Jeffrey and I were both having lunch that day with Aunt Ruthie, Aunt Sylvie, and Uncle Mike. We were meeting them in a restaurant at noon, so we had the morning to talk. I sat around in my bathrobe and told him about Brian. I didn't know what had gone wrong between Brian and me, or even whether I was still in love with him, but I said I wasn't.

Finally I took a shower and got dressed. I was lacing up my shoes—hiking shoes, because I couldn't stand to wear heels so soon after the interview—when Jeffrey wandered back into the living room with a second cup of coffee. He sat in a chair opposite the sofa, listening again, flexing his fingers one at a time, which is what he always does when he listens. "I don't *need* this job," I said, as the phone rang. "I'm not sure I *want* it. But I was good at the interview—clever. *That's* what I need right now—to be Dr. Katz the Clever for a while, not just Annie the not-so-lovable." Jeffrey probably didn't hear my last sentence because he was ambling into the next room to answer the phone, but the call was for me, and was from the youngest doctor in the practice—the one I liked most—who explained that they'd decided not to offer me the position.

I knew the call didn't necessarily mean they hated me. There were plenty of less upsetting explanations—they thought it was polite to be that prompt, or they don't get along and it makes them act funny, and so on. Without saying so, the doctor implied that there was a practical problem, and I was grateful to see it that way, and didn't cry when I hung up. I felt tired, but it was almost time for lunch. Jeffrey kept saying, "Tough, Annie, it's tough," but I insisted I'd be fine if I could just go back to bed and think for a while.

"Do you want me to call them and cancel?" he said.

"Of course not." Obviously it was too late to call. We were meeting at the restaurant, and I knew the relatives had been on their way for a while. They like to leave plenty of time. Finally I did cry, alone in the bathroom, experimentally, but only for a minute. It didn't feel like what I needed.

I didn't like the restaurant, which was someplace in Queens. It had red walls, and red velvet drapes covering the windows. I was afraid my aunts and uncle had picked it because they thought it was what a doctor would prefer. They're all small, dumpy, and plain, and they always seem to wear brown coats. Walking through the phony elegance, they looked even worse. I felt as if we were being told by the restaurant that we were all supposed to be different from what we were, that it was designed that way so we could at least pretend to be different. We were supposed to be ambassadors in an operetta, I decided, people with plumes and shiny buttons. The bright, cold day seemed far away. I wished I was outside.

Still, as the waitress led us single file through the dining room, I was glad to be with Aunt Ruthie, Aunt Sylvie, and Uncle Mike. They were exactly like themselves. Uncle Mike, leading the way, called over his shoulder to me, "Ruthie's got a present for you, Annie, but she's afraid to give it to you"— and Aunt Sylvie, coming last except for Jeffrey, yelled, "Let Ruthie handle it, Mike, would you?" Aunt Ruthie was walking right behind my uncle, her brother-in-law, and she hit him on the shoulder through his coat.

We sat down at a big round table. "You're afraid to give me a present?" I said to Aunt Ruthie. "But I love to get presents." I wished I had a present for her. I hoped she hadn't spent a lot.

"Well, I'm nervous," she said. "I don't know whether you still feel the same way about—you know what."

I realized (with disappointment, oddly, as if I'd expected something I wanted) that the present was going to be picture postcards, and it was. She handed me a package of them— wrapped—across the table.

"Ruthie, would you give the kids a chance to say how they are first?" said Aunt Sylvie.

"No, this is fine," I said. Aunt Ruthie had brought me twenty postcards, an enormous gift. Some looked familiar. I turned one over—a pale, carefully tinted mountain scene. "Dear Joey and Fred," it read in large handwriting. "The weather is good. Mary is afraid to go in the water but I tell her, What would Joey and Fred think? My knee gives me little pain. Yours, Clara."

Aunt Ruthie smiled at me. Her hair is short, straight, thin, still a dull brown. The distance from the smooth top of her head to the glinting chandelier above us made her seem smaller than she is. The ceiling was red too, like the walls and the drapes. I suddenly imagined Brian and the doctors of the day before, rushing toward me in a zigzag line among the tables, bringing me wonderful presents.

"These are fantastic," I said, and put the postcards into my bag.

"You haven't changed," Aunt Sylvie was saying to me. "You still look like a new high-school graduate—you even wear dungarees."

When I'd put on my jeans in the morning I had known she'd make a remark, but I thought it was worth it—I'd just tease her. But now I blurted out, "I might as well be a high-school graduate. I couldn't even get that job." Jeffrey looked up at me quickly. I was surprised too—on the way to the restaurant, I had decided it wouldn't be a lie to pretend I didn't yet know about the job. Now it seemed I might cry.

"The one you came for—the interview was yesterday?" said Aunt Sylvie loudly.

"That's right."

"They told you on the spot?" Aunt Sylvie talked but Aunt Ruthie and Uncle Mike also put down their menus and looked at me, though now the waitress was standing next to Uncle Mike's chair with her pencil poised.

"What happened?" said Aunt Sylvie. "You argued with them?"

"No, of course I didn't," I said, suddenly angry. "I don't know what it was. Look—these things are complicated. It doesn't *mean* anything." I looked straight at the waitress. "I'll have a tuna-fish sandwich and coffee, please," I said.

"Wait a minute, wait a minute," said Aunt Sylvie, as if she were about to announce that nieces who couldn't get jobs didn't get lunch. "Why don't you have the tuna-salad plate? They give you a green salad with the tuna, instead of coleslaw, so it's not just mayonnaise, mayonnaise, mayonnaise."

"Salad plate?" said the waitress.

"No thanks," I said. I snapped my menu closed and put it down.

"And a sandwich is two slices of bread right there," said Aunt Sylvie. She ordered the salad plate, and Aunt Ruthie and the others asked for hamburgers, but then they remembered the job I didn't get. As the waitress walked away, Aunt Ruthie looked at me across the table. "I guess you can't come back to New York," she said quietly, as if we're the same kind of people, she and I—both helpless when it comes to things like fortune.

Sooner or later Uncle Mike always talks about his car, and the one he had last winter was a lemon. He told us for quite a while what was wrong with it—at least it got them off the subject of the job. I even asked questions. Mostly, he said, it wouldn't start.

"How many times have we left you standing in front of your house, Ruthie?" he said. He turned to Jeffrey and me. "We give her a ring and say we're leaving, and then we go out and get in the car—and nothing." Our plates were nearly empty now.

"Which means," Aunt Sylvie said, "disturbing a neighbor, because my foolish sister here won't wait inside where it's warm. So if the car breaks down, she's already out in the street, and the phone doesn't answer. Luckily, Mrs. Aronoff next door is very nice. I call her, and she runs out and tells Ruthie, 'Forget it, they're not coming.' "

Aunt Ruthie looked guilty. "I hate to keep you waiting," she said.

"So how do you think *I* feel, bothering an old lady?" said

Sylvie. "She probably runs outside in her housedress."

"No, no," Ruthie said. "Always a coat over her shoulders. She's very good to me. Everyone is good to me. At work—"

"Drums!" cried Uncle Mike. "Bugles! We're going to hear about Mr. Russo!"

"Her boyfriend," said Aunt Sylvie loudly, but behind her hand, to me.

I looked to see whether Ruthie minded, but she was smiling. I rather liked this turn of the conversation. Ruthie thinking about a man was a new idea.

"Sylvie," she was saying, "he's not my boyfriend. A married man, Catholic, and fifteen years younger. But Anne, if you saw how good he is to me. 'Ruthie,' he'll say, 'take a break. You earned it.' "

"One day," said Uncle Mike in a low voice, "I asked Ruthie to let me pick her up at work, just so I could take a look at this saint, this Mr. Russo." He drew the story out while Ruthie made the same slapping motion that she did when he told me about the present, only this time, since she couldn't reach him, she made it in the air.

"I walked in the door—my heart was beating," he said. "Who knows what I was going to see—Clark Gable? But you know, this Mr. Russo is not so much to look at. Short, fat—"

"Well, *I* think he's good-looking," said Ruthie quickly. "Didn't you see his eyes?"

Aunt Sylvie and Uncle Mike slapped the table and laughed. "But speaking of handsome men," said Aunt Sylvie, turning to me. "How's—what—Bernie? How's that ring finger of yours?"

"Brian," I said. Abruptly, I was at my limit. "He's *fine*." I stood up. "Excuse me. Where's the ladies' room, anyway?"

"I know where it is," said Aunt Ruthie, jumping up. "I have to go too. Come on."

I wished I could be alone for a minute, and as I followed her through the dining room I found I was mentally arguing with my mother, who was telling me my aunts were sweet people who loved me and I was always finding fault with them. We reached the ladies' room, and Aunt Ruthie headed into the second booth, motioning for me to take the first one, still talking about Mr. Russo through the partition between us. I didn't say anything. I felt self-conscious about listening to my aunt urinate, and I didn't feel like talking anyway. Finally, she fell silent, and didn't say anything else until she came out of the booth. I was standing in front of the mirror combing my hair and she started washing her hands, slowly, with soap.

"Annie," she said, "I need to ask you a question." She held her wet hands in the air. "You're a doctor."

I hadn't felt much like a doctor that day. I kept combing my hair.

"I'm embarrassed to mention this," said Aunt Ruthie, "but I think I have a medical problem."

"But I'm a pediatrician," I said, too fast.

"No, I don't mean that. Some things, any doctor can talk about."

"What's wrong with you?" I said. Suddenly I was uneasy in a new way.

"I think I have a lump in my breast."

"How long has it been there?"

"I don't know," said Aunt Ruthie. "I found it a couple of days ago. I saw on television how you should feel your breasts. I didn't know."

"Now don't get panicked," I said. I was enumerating, silently, automatically, "the heart, the liver, the spleen . . ." as though, if I could only remember all I learned in medical school,

I'd get to whatever it was that would help. "You know, it may be nothing," I said.

"I know, I know. I have an appointment with the doctor—My girlfriend at work knows a good doctor. She said the same thing—it might be nothing—my girlfriend."

Aunt Ruthie had been facing me, holding up her wet hands. Now she turned her back and pressed the button on the hot-air drier on the wall. It was noisy. I was standing near the door, rotating the metal clasp on my bag over and over between my fingers. It fits into a slot—when it's vertical, the bag can open; when it's horizontal, the clasp is locked.

"What I need to find out—" said Ruthie. "I have to ask Sylvie and Mike to drive me to the doctor. But—Sylvie—what should I tell her?"

"What should you *tell* her?" I said.

"I can't say I have a lump. Sylvie would think—she'd worry." She looked up at me, her hair tucked behind her ears, her eyes eager. "What should I tell Sylvie is wrong with me, something so she'll think it makes sense to go to that kind of doctor—but not something that will make her worry?"

I wanted to back away—I put my hand out toward the door—but I also didn't want to. "Well—" I began, at last. "This is just as a woman, not as a doctor. But you could say you have a rash in the vagina."

"A rash? . . . Well, that's a good idea. I could just say a rash." Ruthie looked pleased, conspiratorial. "But what about afterward?"

I didn't understand.

"When I come out," Ruthie went on. "What could I say the doctor said?"

"Oh." I shifted my bag a little on my arm. "Well," I said slowly, "I guess he could say it was caused by wearing nylon panties, you know, if they're tight. He might suggest you change to cotton panties." This conversation seemed oddly reminiscent, and then I recognized that it was another interview, and I began to remember yesterday's questions. Maybe this was actually a joke, I thought for a moment, or a dream. . . .

"Really? You think he might say that?" Ruthie looked pleased, as if she thought the doctor might cure the lump in her breast with cotton panties—but then she frowned. "Of course, I may have to tell them the whole story—afterward."

"Ruthie—" I said. I didn't know what to say next, or what to do, and then the door opened and a woman walked past us into a booth.

"Come on," said Aunt Ruthie. "They'll think we flushed ourselves down the toilet."

Uncle Mike took the check. I had whipped out my wallet, but I put it back, mumbling. Jeffrey was able to be gracious, and said, "This is generous of you, Uncle Mike."

But Uncle Mike wasn't sure the check was added up correctly, and he handed it to Aunt Sylvie to look at. "Me?" she said. "The mathematical genius? Einstein?" Then it turned out that Aunt Sylvie can't add without a pencil in her hand, not just to write down the totals, but to make little dots along the side of the column as she works her way down. I searched in my bag and found a pen.

"Exactments," said Jeffrey, smiling at me, after Uncle Mike's long description of Aunt Sylvie's little dots ("Everything, little dots," he said. "The grocery lists. The bookkeeping at the business").

"It's my way," said Aunt Sylvie, looking up from her arithmetic.

"Exactments?" said Aunt Ruthie. "What are exactments?"

I didn't know either. "I was sure you'd remember," Jeffrey said to me. "It's part of my world picture—you don't remember Mr. Palmieri making little dots on the blackboard?"

"No." I persuaded myself that I almost remembered, but I didn't.

"The chemistry teacher at Lane," Jeffrey said. We both went to Franklin K. Lane High School.

"I remember Mr. Palmieri," I said. "I just don't remember any dots."

"When you gave the right answer," Jeffrey said, "he'd say, 'Exactly!' and he'd tap the blackboard with his chalk, and it would make a little dot. At the end of the period there would be all these little dots all over the place. We called them exactments. We used to say, 'I have four exactments.' Once Mark and I signed some."

But Aunt Ruthie still didn't understand. "I never took chemistry," she said. "I took a commercial course. I wouldn't have understood chemistry if I did take it."

"No, it doesn't have to do with chemistry," said Jeffrey. "It could have been any teacher—or anybody."

"It's all right," said Ruthie. "I don't have to understand."

"Yes, you do!" Jeffrey started to explain, and Sylvie and Mike explained, too. Finally Ruthie saw what everybody meant, and explained it back.

"*Exactly!*" we all answered her, and we tapped imaginary blackboards—I too—with imaginary chalk, which we pointed in Aunt Ruthie's direction, as if, in some scrambled way, she'd *turned into* the blackboard. Ruthie loved this routine.

"So if I say to Annie," she said, her voice taking on a professorial depth and timbre, "Annie—" She had to stop and think up a question. "Is Doctor Anne Katz her Aunt Ruthie's *very favorite* doctor? And Annie gives the right answer—" She paused, then whispered fiercely to me, "Give the right answer!"

I shook my head, though I was laughing, but there was no way out, and at last I said, "Yes."

"Then *we* say—"

Now they all said, "Exactly!" in chorus, again, but this time the imaginary chalk was tapping in my direction, and I could bear it for only a moment before I had to wrestle out of their attention, rising above the spot they were smiling at, turning to put on my coat.

The Middle Ages

*T*he mysterious knight, who has known the playwright since she entered the day-care center he attended when she was two, easily slays the dragon and wins the admiration of the princess, whom he has known slightly since she moved into his neighborhood in third grade. The queen makes a congratulatory speech. The knight's mother and the queen's mother exchange looks; they first met eleven years ago, at the screening of the prepared-childbirth film that was to help ready them for the births of the knight and the queen.

The knight asks for a private conference with the king, who shoos the queen and the princess away. The queen, a short white girl, ushers out, in matronly fashion, her tall black daughter. The knight's mother wonders, not for the first time, why the playwright, the strong daughter of a strong mother, writes scenes that depict weak women. Or is this moment in the play because she simply needs to get half her characters off the stage?

The knight, now alone with the king, who has been in this

class with him for two years, confesses that he is not a knight but only a squire. Deeply moved by the courage of his confession, the king does not behead him for impersonation but dubs him a knight "in Christ's name"—a phrase that momentarily startles the knight's Jewish mother, and also, she notes, the playwright's Jewish mother and stepfather. The line seems to go right past the playwright's divorced, non-Jewish father, who is visiting from California. Before the play, he shook hands nostalgically with parents out of his daughter's babyhood, proud to remember their names.

The play ends, and there are congratulations and applause for everyone, including the children who made the costumes and the props. The knight's mother finds her son trying to take off his costume in a corner of the classroom, and goes to help him and hug him. He is noncommittal but seems satisfied with his performance. The group of parents, trooping back into the classroom from the makeshift theater in the school library, address further compliments to the two young teachers—a black man, a white woman—of this Talented and Gifted Class, which has convened on Thursday afternoons all year, gathering children from half the city. It's surprising to the knight's mother, though, how many of them she recognizes, and there are several more whose names she can't remember but who look familiar. The parents move around the room, not sure what is expected of them but happy to catch up on news, to admire the projects on the walls and tables (all connected with the Middle Ages), to smile shyly and exchange pleasantries with the families they do not know.

The knight's mother walks slowly around the tables, looking at the castles. They are made of plain cardboard and corrugated cardboard, along with toilet-paper rolls, paper-towel rolls, string, tape, and sections of egg cartons. One has a drawbridge with string cables to draw it up. Crouching, she sees that another castle has been divided into rooms. The labor is intricate. She sees little clay sheep and geese in a courtyard; there is a tilting clay woman mounting a cardboard staircase, which seems to want to straighten itself. The knight's castle is the smallest in the classroom and one of the simplest, but it has crenellated walls, meticulously cut.

The man teacher comes to talk to her about the castles. The children worked in groups, he explains. The groups were varied, and the teachers were careful to place children with classmates they didn't know very well. The knight worked with one other child, a girl, which must not have been easy for him. They agree that the knight is shy with girls. At first, he was in a larger group, the teacher explains, but one child was difficult, and the teachers thought it best to divide this group. The mother remembers that the knight talked about the difficult child, and about the castle, but not about a girl.

The teacher is proud of the way the castles were made. He explains that one of the children, on her end-of-the-year Program Evaluation Sheet, actually wrote that it was her favorite project because she learned to work with different kinds of children. The mother and the teacher agree that this result was indeed praiseworthy.

The knight's mother now introduces the knight's grandmother to the director of the Talented and Gifted Program, a woman famous for her memory, who mentions the occasion on which she met the grandmother before, at another Medieval Fair, three years ago, when the knight's older brother was in fifth grade. No, the brother is not here tonight; he is playing the cello in an ensemble at the music school. His father dropped him off and was almost late for the play. The older brother did not seem to mind that his parents were missing his concert.

They have attended others—long, earnest performances by a succession of small groups. Each time, the father wondered whether some young virtuoso might save the occasion.

But now the knight's mother begins to worry, imagining the music-school concert over and the audience dispersed, her son alone in the dark with his cello outside a locked building, or perhaps being conscientiously kept company by the already exhausted teacher.

The knight explains that they cannot leave. He may be allowed to take his castle home. At the last class, the teachers asked the children in each group to draw lots for the group's castle. He and his co-worker, Jonquil McMahon, drew lots and Jonquil won. But she is not present. "If the first person doesn't come by a quarter to nine, the second person can take the castle," the knight says. "I'm the second person, because there isn't anybody else." It is now eight-twenty. Families are beginning to leave. The fathers, supervised by anxious sons and daughters, carefully detach large medieval figures painted on brown wrapping paper from the wall—knights, ladies, monks—loosening the Scotch tape piece by piece and trying to keep the arms and legs from tearing.

Each student has made a coat of arms, a cardboard shield divided into four sections. The knight explains that one quarter of each coat of arms represents the present, one the future, one something he is proud of, and one something he enjoys. To show the present, he has drawn his family, including the cat and dog. A scroll surprisingly lettered PH.D. IN LITERATURE denotes his future. He is proud of his certificate for cooperation, from summer day camp. Pleasure is shown by a hockey stick. The knight's mother picks out herself, with dark hair, in the row of family members. She cannot remember ever making anything like this coat of arms, a work that might acknowledge and unite the parts of her life.

By the time the coat of arms has been taken down and examined, it is eight-thirty. One of the teachers thinks the knight might take the castle now, but the other teacher says they should not deviate from the announced plan. The knight, in any case, has no wish to break the rules. He sits at a table in the library with his mother and grandmother. The father stays in the classroom, restlessly moving around, picking up books about the Middle Ages. The mother can see him through the doorway. She recognizes the book he has been looking at. When she passed the table and glanced at it, it was opened to a detailed description of medieval warfare, including the use of boiling oil.

"Is Jonquil a black girl?" asks the grandmother.

"Yes."

"I like the name Jonquil," says the mother.

"She looks like what you'd think," the knight says.

"Delicate?"

"Sort of."

"I feel sorry for her," says the grandmother. "Maybe she wanted to come but she couldn't."

"I don't think she wanted to come," says the knight.

At twenty-five to nine, the mother goes back into the classroom. Two or three families are left. The teachers are starting to take down from the walls the work of the children who didn't show up. The playwright's father has gone, taking with him the playwright's life-size cutout on brown paper of a lady in a conical hat; perhaps he means to take it back to California with him. Now the playwright's mother and stepfather take their leave with the playwright, the mother carrying the playwright's new baby brother, the stepfather balancing one of the largest castles, which he tilts carefully to fit it through the door.

The knight has come back into the classroom. He is watching the clock. The mother sits down on the corner of a table. She thinks she should keep the grandmother company in the library, but she isn't wearing a watch and wants to know what time it is. Across the room, the father has found something to read. It looks like a storybook, with a colorful cover. He is leaning with one shoulder against a blackboard, holding the book a little away from him, as if he means to be able to drop it at any moment.

"Six and a half minutes," the knight says.

"That's *you*," says the woman teacher, smiling at the knight. "You really are a stickler for rules. Everything just so. But you're such a good judge. You make us all be fair in class. And you never take anything you're not entitled to."

The knight shrugs. He does not recognize himself in the description.

"Four minutes," says the knight. The father is impatient. He closes the book and puts it down. Obviously, Jonquil is not coming. The fair is over. They discuss carrying the castle out to the car. Or should he drive around to the door? No, he answers himself, they can carry the castle easily. But the bottom is paper, not cardboard. Will the walls make it rigid enough? Can they carry it without hurting it?

"I really think you can take it now," says the woman teacher.

"No. A minute to go," the knight says.

"You're a little crazy," she says. "But it's a good kind of crazy."

The knight is staring at the clock. The mother is standing up, tired, her face empty. A last family is leaving. Another family is walking into the classroom—a woman, a teenage girl, a younger girl: a black family. They look calm, as if they are doing something ordinary.

The mother sees that this is not a family that has been here all evening, returning for a forgotten picture or jacket. This is Jonquil.

The woman teacher, her eyes startled, is greeting the teenage sister—another former student, it seems. The knight's family does not wait to see Jonquil—who is expressionless and sturdy, not delicate—take up the castle. The mother feels the knight yank at her arm. They hurry the grandmother out to the car.

"It would have been worse if we'd met them in the street and had to deal with an ethical dilemma," says the mother as they start down the steps outside the building.

"They looked cynical," says the father. "This was terrible. This was truly terrible."

The grandmother says that maybe the family had no choice but to come late, that they had to be somewhere else. It is the end of the school year. There are many celebrations and performances. The concert, for example.

"That's not how they looked," says the mother. She tries to picture the woman's businesslike face wearing the expression that all mothers—housewives or working women, black or white—wear when they rush in late to claim a child or to applaud and admire: the exasperated eyes, the frustrated headshake that says "Of *course* I care. It was traffic, responsibility, necessity that kept me away—not ease, not whim."

The face, in the mother's mind, will not hold the expression. The woman did not want to make the usual half-humorous claim of membership in the guild of the conscientious, or did not know she could. Or perhaps for her an avowal of fellowship would be a mad luxury, courtly protocol in the midst of battle.

The mother doesn't know how to explain this to the boy but reaches out a hand, as they approach the car, to touch the back of his neck. He brushes his head against her palm, and she thinks he may turn and cry, but he does not.

"Still," says the grandmother, "now you know how to make castles."

"I couldn't get the wall to stand up straight," says the boy. "Mr. Evans had to glue it for me, and then he told me it came apart after I went home and he had to glue it again. I didn't know what to do. It kept on falling."

The May Dance

Jan has been home alone with her younger son, William, all this Saturday morning, trying to clean a little and to get him through page 137. William hasn't done any math homework for two weeks, and he's five assignments behind in reading. Page 137 is in his reader, at the end of a story about an American girl living during the Revolutionary War who infiltrates the British lines disguised as her grandfather, a doctor. Jan has looked over the story, but hasn't read it, though William has—that part is easy for him.

Starting near the top of the page, after the last few sentences of the story, are "Questions for Discussion and Thought." William's teacher wants the children to answer these questions in writing, and then, also, to write answers to a second group of questions designated "Writing About What You've Learned." Both kinds of questions follow each story in the book, but sometimes a story ends closer to the bottom of a page than on page 137, and there isn't room for very many altogether. Then, too, the proportion varies. Jan always hopes there will be fewer

"Discussion and Thought" questions—they're vaguer, or something; William has more trouble with them. On page 137, though, there are only two questions under "Writing About What You've Learned," but *five* under "Discussion and Thought"; and not only that—one of them is broken up into parts a, b, and c.

Today it was hard even to get William to write his name at the top of his notebook page. Jan would come through the kitchen, where he was supposedly working, every so often, and discover that in ten minutes he'd added only three letters to his name—then he'd wandered off. He'd be standing on a chair—lately, William stands on chairs. "Mommy," he said once, as she came into the room, "some people think dinosaurs only ate plants, but that's wrong, because many of them were carnivores."

"How about that?" But she was already impatient. She looked at the first question, which read, "In what ways was Matilda like children of her age in the twentieth century and in what ways was she different? Are these ways important to you? Why or why not?"

"William," said Jan, "I know this is irritating. But you have to do it. Look. Just tell me *one* way that Matilda was like a modern kid."

"She peed," said William.

"It says that?"

"No," said William, "but she was a human being, wasn't she?"

When her sister Robin rings the doorbell, William is only on the second question. Jan has sat down opposite him. She knows that's a mistake—she can only succeed when she is busy with something else, just glancing at him, keeping her voice light.

"William," she is saying, with more anger than she expected, "*please* pick up the pencil. No. Sit down. Come on. Now *pick up* the pencil—" The doorbell rings and she is released. She strides to the door to let Robin in—and when they come back, William is standing on a chair again.

Robin comes with her arms full, cradling a large brown paper bag from Horowitz Brothers, the fabric store—a used bag, reticulated and limp with creases, and containing the parts of the dress she's been working on—or not working on, as she explained when she called last night and asked Jan to help her make it. She's short, broad-shouldered, with long straight blond hair, and when Jan opens the door she is looking surprised.

"I remembered my dream," she says, "*just* as I pushed the doorbell. I dreamed about you last night."

"Hi," says Jan.

"We were getting married," says Robin. She follows Jan to the kitchen. "To each *other*. We were sewing—this must come from calling you up last night. We were making our wedding gowns. Mine was pink and yours was blue."

"Of course," says Jan. When they were children, Robin's towel was always pink and hers was blue—she still buys blue nightgowns, blue toothbrushes.

"But in the *dream*," continues Robin, "nobody thought it was *strange* that we were marrying each other—it was just sort of— incompetent."

"Oh," says Jan. "I've had dreams like that—"

"In the dream," says Robin, "it was as if marrying your sister was like using Cool Whip instead of making real whipped cream. Hi, Willie."

Jan puts up water to boil for coffee. She can almost remember a dream—the same *kind* of dream, in which everyone seems to know that an event's meaning is not at all what it would be in waking life. She's lost the energy that could make William work—somehow she doesn't want to try in front of Robin. She doesn't care whether he ever does his homework. Then, seconds later, she does care—but she knows that what will work is detachment. She must forget about it—though of course it was her forgetting about it that got William this far behind in the first place.

"You're late," she says to Robin.

"I know," says Robin. "Does it matter? I'm depressed."

"I don't mind," says Jan. "But we have to leave in a while. There's a thing at the school. William is in the maypole dance."

"That's all right—I'll go too," says Robin. "Didn't you know I'd want to go?"

"Yes, but the dress," says Jan. "You said it mattered."

"Oh, it does," says Robin. She starts taking the parts of the dress out of the bag. She's cut them all out, and the tan tissue-paper sections of the pattern are still pinned to the pieces of fabric, but some of them have come off at a corner, or are wrinkled or torn. Jan picks up a piece labeled BACK and tries to smooth it. She looks at the drawing on the pattern envelope. The dress is in an old-fashioned style with puffed sleeves, a yoke, and a wide skirt, and Robin is making it in pink calico with tiny flowers all over it.

"Pink, huh?" says Jan. Robin laughs, and hums "Here Comes the Bride," pacing deliberately around the kitchen.

"William," says Jan, feeling better, "how about sitting down and showing Aunt Robin how fast you can work? Robin, have you ever seen this speed demon here do homework?"

"No," says William. "I'm not doing it."

"How come he has to do homework on Saturdays?" says Robin. "Homework's for Sunday night, starting after supper. Right, Willie?"

"Because he's weeks behind," Jan says. "Because I have in

my pocket a *signed contract* scheduling his whole weekend, which is the only possible way he can get caught up. As he knows."

"Well, I'm not doing it," says William.

"Your mom hasn't changed, Willie," says Robin. "*She* always did homework on Saturday morning. Or Friday afternoon. I couldn't *stand* it. *I* never did homework at all." William, standing on a chair, looks from one sister to the other.

"Oh, I did not," says Jan. "Enough of this," she says sharply to William. "Now, *get started*." Her voice is suddenly harsh. William bursts into tears and runs out of the room.

The dress front must be gathered across the top edge, and then sewn to the two halves of the yoke. Robin had attached one half, but the gathers weren't even, and so it bunched. Jan has spent the last half hour ripping it out. She doesn't sew very well herself, but she's had a little more experience than Robin.

"I love this dress," says Robin. "I saw one like it in a catalog, and it was incredibly expensive. I thought, Well, I could make that."

Jan has brought the sewing machine from an upstairs closet, and is setting it up. It probably should be oiled, but that would take forever. She clears a larger space on the table. William's books are in the way. She knows he won't come back, but just in case, she moves his book and notebook to a chair without losing the place, the pencil resting in the middle of the book, which is still open to the right page.

Robin makes herself a second cup of coffee. She's turned on the stove and is leaning against the counter next to it, her back to Jan, staring out the window. It's May, and Jan can see the lilacs in her backyard, patchy and scraggly but glorious in spots, outdoing themselves this year.

"I like purple too, not just pink," says Robin. She must be

looking at the lilacs, too. "I'm depressed about work," she says. For a few months, Robin has worked in the billing department of a hospital. "I had a fight with Barry."

Jan finds the spool of pink thread among Robin's belongings, and starts to fill up a bobbin. "What happened?" she says.

"I got my evaluation," says Robin. "Of course I knew it wouldn't be good because of Marilyn. It couldn't be as good as *Marilyn's.*"

"I forget which one is Marilyn."

"She's the one who flutters over to Barry three times a day." Robin's voice turns fluty. " 'Now I just thought I ought to *consult* with you, Barry, before I sent this out, just in case there's some *aspect* that hasn't *occurred* to me—' "

"Oh, right." Jan gets the machine threaded.

The water boils and Robin goes rummaging in the cupboard for the instant coffee. "I see myself doing it," she says. "First I'm going to screw up the little things, then the big things."

"Wait a minute," says Jan. "What happened with the evaluation?"

"Oh, it doesn't really matter," says Robin. "I got it on Tuesday. The only thing that surprised me was that that woman, Mrs. Reilly—you know, she just gets a paragraph at the bottom—she said I had 'attitude problems.' I don't even know what she's talking about."

"Did you go and ask her?"

"There's no *point,*" says Robin. "Anyway, on Wednesday, Barry asked me to make some calls for him, and I was busy. I got mad, and I said some things I probably shouldn't have."

Jan is sewing the front to the yoke of the dress. There is an opening on top where there will be facings and buttons later. It isn't a simple dress, really.

"Have you tried to talk it over with him?" But her voice sounds wrong, even to her.

"No," says Robin. "Really, I'm so tired of that stuff. 'Just *talk* it *over*—and you can fix *anything*.'" Exaggerating the gesture, as if in imitation of someone, she waves her hand dismissively. Then she spreads the instructions out on the table. "We should probably try and skip some of these steps or something—but I know you won't let me. The spirit that made you do homework on Fridays, I guess."

Jan doesn't answer. She knows they can't skip any steps. She's sure she didn't do homework on Fridays. She does remember doing it once, on a Friday, one single time—and how delightful it felt to be free for the weekend—but the memory itself proves, surely, that it wasn't her habit.

They stop for sandwiches, after a while, but then it is almost time to walk over to the school. The Spring Fair is going on there all day, but William has refused to participate in the morning's events—games, exhibits, a plant sale. Anyway, it seemed like a good time, with Jan and William alone—Jan's husband and their older son, Stephen, are off camping with the Boy Scouts for the weekend—to get the homework done.

But that plan certainly hasn't worked. She's passed the open door to William's room twice since he went upstairs. At first, he was lying face down on the bed. She tried to talk to him, but he wouldn't answer. Later he was on the floor, playing with Lego and talking to himself, so she relaxed a bit.

All the children in the school perform folk dances at the annual fair. There's a simple round dance that's done by the kindergarten, and a dance of couples in a line, one pair bouncing down and back, which is carried off, with high spirits and only a little scrambling, by the second grade. William is in the fourth grade, the oldest group, this year, and the fourth grade always dances around the maypole, though William doesn't know whether he is to be one of the ribbon *holders,* who, though terribly important, are still faintly secondary personages—or one of the ribbon dancers themselves. In rehearsals, he has explained, they take turns. Jan thought William might refuse to dance altogether, since he has refused to do almost everything anyone has asked of him lately—but he has talked about the maypole with casual pride, the way Stephen did three years ago.

"It won't take long," she says to Robin. "We can work some more when we get back."

They've now attached the front to the back of the dress, at the shoulders, and sewn up the side seams. The sleeves aren't in yet, but it's time for Robin to try the dress on. She takes off her jeans and shirt, and slips the unfinished dress on over her head. It's intensely pink—flowery and wide. Robin moves over to the mirror in the hall and studies herself critically. "I look like I need a crook and two lambs," she says. William appears, leaning over the banister, halfway down the stairs.

"It makes me look a little heavy," says Robin.

"Yes," says William. "You look like a laundry bag."

Robin is only slightly overweight, but the dress does seem to make that more obvious. Before she thinks, Jan gives an appreciative snort.

"A lot of work for nothing, I guess," says Robin wearily.

"Oh, *no,*" says Jan, sure she must disagree before she knows what she'll say. "It just needs a belt." She hurries into the kitchen, finds a long, narrow scrap, and ties it, sash style, around her sister's waist—but the dress still billows out above and below it.

"Now you look like two laundry bags," says William.

"William, that's rude, and it's *not true*," says Jan, wheeling around to face him, yet aware that if she scolds him too hard, he'll hide himself away and miss the dancing. He turns and runs back upstairs, and she hears his door slam.

"*Now* you say it," says Robin. "When it's too late."

"Oh, Robin, I'm sorry that happened," says Jan. "But listen—loose dresses always look like that when they're half done. It'll be different when it's hemmed and all."

"I don't see what the hem has to do with it," says Robin. "I'm fat, that's all. I *know* I'm gaining weight." She smooths the dress over her hips. "Or you're trying to make me *feel* fat. I don't know why it gives you pleasure to hit me where I'm weakest. God knows what unfinished business you're working out on me." She stands there in the huge pink dress, her bare arms hanging heavily at her sides. Then she bends down, crosses her arms, and grasps the bottom edge with both hands—a child's gesture—to take the dress off. As Jan watches, it comes up and goes over Robin's head, and then Robin turns away, in her bra and panties, to find her clothes, letting the dress fall to the floor inside out. Jan picks it up and turns it right side out.

"Hey," she says. "You're not breaking off our engagement, are you?"

"Look, that dream had nothing to do with our actual relationship," says Robin. "Anyone can see that. And I really don't feel like joking." She puts on her shirt and pants, buttons the shirt, and tucks it in, sucking in her stomach to button the pants waist and zip up the fly. "At least I'll see Willie dance," she says. "When Stephen did it, you didn't let me know."

Jan is glad that Robin still wants to go along, and relieved when she calls to William and he, too, appears, though he's walking slowly and looking like an emblem of anger, his arms folded, a frown carefully fixed on his forehead. But Robin is packing all the parts of the dress back into the ancient brown paper bag and whipping her spool of pink thread off the spindle of Jan's machine.

"Please don't be angry," Jan says to her. "Let's finish it later."

"I'm not angry," says Robin. "But frankly, I have a lot to do this weekend. I have to take some things to the cleaners before it closes—I'm going to make time for the dancing, because I know it's important to Willie, but I have a lot I need to accomplish today." Robin lives only a few blocks beyond the school, which itself is three blocks away. She came on foot this morning. Now she folds her arms around the brown bag and they all set out, walking, though William won't catch up to them, and Jan is uneasy about him all the way, thinking he may suddenly stop, and stay stopped.

It's an old, square, dull-brick public school with a blacktop yard in back, now colorful with balloons and crafts. In the center of the yard is the maypole, tall and sturdy, on a base cleverly fitted with wheels so it can be moved to and from the storage room. It was made several years ago by a committee of parents—one of them told Jan how they'd stood there, listening to the music teacher explain, for a long time, and then they knew what she wanted. From the top of the pole come ribbons, maybe twenty, half green and half yellow.

Jan, with Robin silent at her side, has been talking to the kindergarten teacher, who says she can hardly believe that William is in the maypole group already, that it seems so recently that he was her pupil. "You never could tell what he'd say," she recalls, excusing herself to go check on her class. While Jan has been talking, the children have all gone into the school to get ready, and now the parents are gathering at the edges of the playground to wait for the dancing. At some point, some of the oldest children have come out and taken hold of the ribbons of the maypole. They are sitting in a tight group, cross-legged, around the pole, and one girl is standing, her arms full of flowers—the Queen of the May. All these children, Jan notices, have wreaths of flowers—white, yellow, purple—around their heads, and they all have white shirts or blouses on. William, today, is wearing a red-and-blue sweater, a little dingy for want of laundering, with reindeers on it. He never told her about white shirts. She doesn't see him among the children around the pole.

Now the whole school parades out, marching to a country dance played on a fiddle and a flute by somebody's mother and somebody else's older brother. The littlest children come first. Jan and Robin move to see better.

The children come out in lines that turn formless as they arrive at the steps, one group after another. The maypole dancers are last, all in white shirts—except for one boy in green plaid—all with wreaths circling their heads. William isn't there.

Jan knows the teachers wouldn't keep him out because of his sweater—such a notion would make the music teacher cry, and there she is, directing things—eyes bright, laughing. He has probably refused to wear a wreath—Jan cannot imagine anyone putting a wreath on William—and though she knows *that* wouldn't faze the teachers here either ("He's a *sensitive child*," they're always reminding her), she thinks it might faze William. Maybe he is sobbing in a corner of his classroom, not allowing himself to dance sweatered and wreathless. Jan wonders whether she should go in and look for him.

"He can't stop wriggling," says Robin.

"Who can't?"

"Willie."

"Where? I can't find him."

"He's behind the pole." Now she sees him. William and his sweater have been hidden from her by another child's head and the pole itself. She shifts her own head to see him better. He's wearing a wreath.

"God, it's hot," says Robin.

The younger children dance and sing. Their voices are serious, old-fashioned, true—but they move easily and loosely, the way they do at recess when they chase each other through this yard. Jan recognizes most of the dances—one year or another, her children have done them all. The dancers grow gradually taller and then it's time for the maypole dance. The children holding the ribbons stand and begin to move to the flute and fiddle, doing a preliminary dance with bowing and marching.

"He's a ribbon holder," says Jan. "He won't get to weave—he's just in the first part."

It doesn't seem to matter. William is solemn—maybe a little sulky—but he moves in step like the other children, and, at the end of his part of the dance, hands over his green ribbon with a flourish to a white-shirted boy who steps forward from the surrounding circle.

Now there's a pause in the music, and the ribbon holders take their places outside the circle. The music begins again, and the new dancers space themselves in as wide a circle as possible, the green and yellow ribbons radiating around the pole.

The dance tantalizes at first—the dancers step forward, then back, slip under one another's ribbons, then, again, back. You think—Jan thinks, though she's seen it before—that you haven't understood, that they will just move the ribbons about and stop. Then the music takes hold of its theme again, and the dancers step sturdily forward, some facing one way with yellow ribbons, some the other way, with green. Now you see what they are doing, with their grave and courteous dipping and reaching, stepping under one another's outstretched arms, carrying their ribbons carefully across one another's backs. As the fiddle and flute play and the children dip and reach, a green and yellow fabric, evenly checkered, forms itself from nothing around the top of the pole, and continues to form itself, a strange, lovely thing woven up high, out of everyone's reach.

The parents cheer and clap and the music stops. The children stop. The ribbons are shorter now, and the green and yellow weaving runs a foot down the pole.

"Look, I have to get out of here," says Robin, putting her hand on Jan's arm for a moment, almost as if Jan were blocking her way. She waves the same hand toward the children—"Terrific"; then she thrusts her way through the crowd, squeezing her paper bag. Jan turns and sees her walk away from the schoolyard, down the street, with long strides.

But the music teacher has signaled to start the fiddling and flute playing again and when Jan looks back, she sees something she doesn't remember—the dance is going the other way, so the children are unraveling what they have woven. The weaving is loosening and disappearing, and the ribbons are becoming long again.

She doesn't think she's seen the children do this before, but of course they always must, it occurs to her—how else could they prepare the pole to be used again? She doesn't know why the music teacher is having them unravel the weaving now, with the fiddle playing and parents watching, but it must be what always happens on the Monday morning after the fair, the children in their ordinary jeans and T-shirts, the playground empty of balloons and applause.

The program has been long, and the sun *is* warm. Still, the teacher conducts and the music continues, and now Jan sees that it is not over at all, because the ribbon holders—William too—have come forward once more, taken the newly freed ribbons, and stepped with suppressed excitement into the circle around the pole.

So that's it—this year, everyone may weave. Jan wishes she could bring her sister back with the news, and she even looks to see whether perhaps Robin has changed her mind and is coming toward them again, but she is not. Again, the new children step teasingly back and forth. They don't smile—they're intent; the steps are complicated. Now they weave, and the teacher doesn't stop them even when the green and yellow fabric around the pole creeps far down, and the ribbons grow short. When William goes past Jan at first, she sees that he is working hard not to smile—then he is smiling—but the teacher is a funny, loving lady who lets the children dance until they're all laughing, William and the others, and the pole is all green and yellow, the ribbons so short that the children are crowded together, almost woven into the pattern, which is bright with the purple, yellow, and white flowers in their hair, and with *them*. It's a shout at the darkness of May.

Sleeping Giant

"Charlotte's having an adventure," says Laura to Dan, her husband. "She's exploring. Look." Charlotte has recently learned to walk, but she sometimes falls forward and crawls for a few steps. She's wearing lightweight overalls and a short-sleeved shirt—it's a breezy day in August—but the bumpy ground she's on doesn't seem to bother her. They are all in the picnic grounds at Sleeping Giant State Park, and Laura is sitting on a bench at a picnic table, her back to the table, drinking red wine. She stretches out her legs so a square of sunlight that's penetrating the trees can reach them. The warmth is welcome, coming through the denim of her jeans, though in a few minutes it will be too much. Now Charlotte, who is Laura and Dan's grand-child, sits down hard, her legs stuck out in front of her, and brings a handful of dry pine needles to her mouth, then drops them, rolls over onto her hands and knees, stands, and walks meditatively away from them, tipping first to one side and then to the other, looking tiny and solitary—in pink—among the long gray trunks of the pine trees.

Dan is lighting the fire in the grill. He's behind Laura, whistling a sad song. She can tell when he lifts something, or stretches—pouring the charcoal from a heavy sack, straightening up and reaching back to the picnic table for the can of charcoal lighter and the box of matches—because the tune, his usual one for slow action, breaks off.

Helen and Mitchell, their daughter and son-in-law, are shopping—it's Mitchell's birthday, and they're buying him a present. They will meet Laura and Dan here for lunch, birthday cake, and a walk up to the tower, a satisfying stone structure on one of the hills—it *seems* old and storied, though it has no obvious purpose. Laura has looked forward to the day. She's been troubled about Mitchell lately—she's never been entirely untroubled about him—but, she said to Dan, she could cheerfully make an effort for his birthday—"I can celebrate his *birth*. New Mitchell." And so she'd worked in the kitchen all morning.

"How hungry are you?" says Dan. He has lit the fire and is sitting back on his heels watching the flames flare and die down.

Laura laughs. "I can wait," she says. Their cookouts are always slow. But she moves over to the picnic basket, still watching Charlotte, and starts taking things out. They're making shish kebabs, and she'd already cut up mushrooms, onions, and green peppers, and marinated the cubes of beef. Now she finds the skewers and starts sliding chunks of meat and slices of green pepper and onions into place. Shadows intersect on the table, and in the moving sunlight, the slices of vegetable look, each of them, fresh and rich in color. She hears a car, glances at Charlotte, who is tossing handfuls of pine needles into the air, and then looks—but it's a green car, and her daughter and son-in-law's car is blue.

"I don't know what he wants from me," she says, looking

back at the vegetables. "I can't stop him—*or* give him permission."

"Mitchell? He wants you to think it's a good idea."

"He ought to know I can't help what I think. But he won't leave me alone." Mitchell has come into some money after his father's death. He wants to buy a two-family house in New Haven, move his family out of the rented house where they now live and into one apartment, and renovate the house himself with the aid of a mortgage and a bank loan. Then he will sell it—at a profit, he claims, large enough to pay off the loans and allow him and Helen to buy another house to live in—a bigger, finer house than they could afford now.

"I suppose it might work out," says Dan.

"You know it won't," Laura says. "Mitchell thinks he's this old-world carpenter who's going to perform wonders on a historical gem. But he doesn't know anything. All those projects of his—"

"It's really not that," Dan says. "Lots of people don't know much. But Mitchell—well, he'll ask my advice and thank me over and over, and then whatever I suggest—it just happens the hardware store is out of it. I'd rather he'd fight with me."

"Besides," says Laura, "that house—those dark little rooms . . . Just bringing that house up to *code*—" She slides a mushroom onto a skewer and it splits, so she eats it, turning around to look at Dan's back, and reaches for another one. "When I tried to talk to Helen," she continues, "she just said she thought I liked creative people."

"Helen sees your point of view," says Dan. "Don't worry."

"I don't think she does."

"I know she does," says Dan. "She talked about it the other day. She's afraid he just won't get the work done. He'll be at the office and she'll be in chaos with the baby." Dan squats and pokes the coals. "Believe me, she's not happy about this."

"Well, why doesn't she tell him so?"

He doesn't answer.

"What did she say *exactly*?" Laura is searching in her canvas tote bag for her car keys. She's chilly after all, and there's a flannel shirt in the trunk of the car. She waits, holding the keys and the bag, but Dan still doesn't answer, and she drops the bag on the bench. "What did she *say*?"

"Oh, I don't remember. General things."

"What did *you* say?"

"Oh, I don't know, Laura." Laura turns aside abruptly, opens the trunk, and stares into it for a moment, annoyed that Dan won't tell her more, before she remembers the flannel shirt. But when she's thrust her arms into the sleeves and banged the trunk lid closed, and she turns—keys in hand, feeling better, trying to think where she put the bag—Charlotte is dragging it away from the bench, pulling it along the ground by one red canvas handle. Laura steps toward her and Charlotte looks up, interested, drops the bag, and tries to pick it up again, but this time she grasps it at the bottom, so that everything in it spills onto the ground. "Oh, *no*," Laura says quickly—then, crouching, "It's OK, Char—it's my fault. I shouldn't have left it there." She sits down, talking to Charlotte as if the baby could understand, and starts gathering things, and Dan quickly stretches out a foot to capture a scrap of paper that's blowing away. He picks it up, and then bends to poke through the dry leaves and pine needles for Laura's other possessions.

"I should have watched her," says Laura. She leans over to Charlotte and takes her comb away, and then she spots her pen under the pine needles and digs in for it. The needles are smooth and light, and the ground underneath them is damp and cool. Laura scoops up needles and sifts them through her fingers, and Charlotte imitates her—it's not too different from what she was doing before, Laura sees. Charlotte laughs when the pine needles fall on her, and gathers them in fistfuls, and, a minute later, they are all still sitting like that when Mitchell and Helen's blue car comes slowly up the drive and eases to a stop next to theirs.

"What's this, a game?" says Helen, coming toward them. She has a red scarf tied around her hair; her face looks round and earnest.

"Oh, I lost track of her, yapping at your father," says Laura. "She spilled my purse."

"She's into everything these days," says Helen, kneeling to help.

Mitchell brushes off Laura's bag and holds it open so that everyone can put into it what has been gathered—wallet, old letters, pencils. Then he hands it back to Laura with a ceremonial dip of the head. "Do you want to see my present?" he says.

He's a tall man, and though they've all scrambled to their feet he almost stoops to talk to Laura. She says she'd like to see it. It's a handsome tweed sport coat for fall, and Laura and Dan admire it. Mitchell models it for them. Then he puts away the new jacket and gets busy, carrying the shish kebabs to Dan (though the fire isn't quite ready yet), pouring more wine for Laura.

Helen comes over to her. "Where's the back carrier?" she asks. "If I put Charlotte in now, and walk around, maybe she'll nap."

The back carrier—Laura looks quickly from the bench to the car, as if it were subject to conjuring—but she knows where it is: on her kitchen table at home, where Helen had left it this morning. "You might need this," she'd said. "You won't forget it if I put it right here next to the cake. We can use it for the walk up to the tower." But Laura had forgotten. Dan had carried the baby and the picnic basket out to the car, and Laura had looked around the kitchen, holding the cake on its plate. She'd stared right at the carrier, she supposes, but didn't see it—she'd been rushed just then, and busy talking, trying to make some point or other to Dan. "Matches?" Dan had said. "Baby food? Corkscrew?"

"I'm sorry," she says now. "I guess we won't be able to walk up to the tower." But it would have been wonderful, the exercise in the bright air, the view—

"Oh, we can carry her," says Helen.

"Helen, I'm losing my marbles."

"No, you've just got your mind on the intangibles, Mom."

Laura sits down with her wine, and watches as her daughter sets to work getting the paper plates ready while whispering nonsense to Charlotte, who is standing near the bench chewing a piece of bread. Usually Laura is the busy one, but she shouldn't be *allowed* to take charge of things, she thinks—she's too careless, too restless and critical. Helen is lovely with the baby, simple and quiet—and now Dan takes Charlotte and holds her peacefully against his shoulder, walking up and down under the trees, whistling again.

Her son-in-law brings her a plate of food. "Leave room for that cake now!" he says, as if Laura hadn't been the one who baked it.

The shish kebabs are excellent. Mitchell eats two, though they're big ones, and then hurries the group on to the birthday cake. Laura had remembered candles. It's a chocolate cake with jam between the layers, and chocolate icing—she wasn't sure the combination would work, but it did. Charlotte eats a little, but she's tired now, and wants to be held. Yet when Mitchell picks her up, she reaches for Helen, and then she won't let Helen carry her either, but wrestles loose to run unsteadily away from the adults around her. "She can walk a little," says Helen. "She'll get so tired she'll *have* to let someone hold her." They've put the picnic things into the cars, which will be left here during the climb. Now they move toward the start of the trail, at the edge of the picnic ground. Laura, who's jumpy, too full of birthday cake, forces herself to walk slowly beside Helen, who is holding Charlotte's hand. The trail is level at first, moving in and out of the shade into the sun. Dan and Mitchell start off together at a normal pace, and almost immediately are far ahead of the women on the tower trail, which is just smooth and wide enough for ordinary walking in ordinary shoes, unlike the more serious hiking trails that wind and crisscross through this large park.

Charlotte takes a few steps, but she keeps stopping or falling, and Helen must soothe her every few feet. Finally Laura can wait no longer. She picks up the baby and strides forward, holding her across her hip. Charlotte kicks, but Laura doesn't give in. Helen hurries after them, calling, "Oh, Charlotte, honey, let Grandma carry you—" Then Laura sees Mitchell running down the path toward them.

"I'll take her," he says tautly. "Helen, you shouldn't let your mother carry her. She's heavy. And I don't know *why* you can't get her quiet." He seizes Charlotte, sits her on his shoulders, her legs dangling down onto his chest, and grasps her ankles. She cries, though she holds on to Mitchell's head as he walks back up the path toward Dan, but it's the sort of hard crying, Laura knows, that will finally let her give up and fall asleep.

Laura turns to Helen, unable to keep silent. "That was *awful*—" she begins, but Helen breaks in, "Oh, he's just nervous.

It's nothing." Then she begins to talk cheerfully about the morning, how they had to go to several stores before they could find what they wanted. In one place, Mitchell almost bought a jacket in a bold plaid that Helen disliked. "Mitchell's so proud of his 'eye,' as he puts it," she says. "I couldn't just say it was ugly."

"What *did* you say?"

"I pretended I was Dad. I knew if I did that, the right words would come. I said it was 'Just possibly . . .'" She draws her words out. " 'Possibly . . .' I never got to 'possibly' *what*. I just kept looking doubtful, and finally he said it pulled under his arms."

"Possibly impossible, I guess," says Laura with a laugh.

"Oh, no, it was *definitely* impossible," says Helen, smiling—but then quiet.

They have gone about halfway up. The hill they are climbing rises beside them on their right, and to the left, below them, is a narrow valley, almost a gorge, walled by a wooded cliff that is just far away enough so that if there were people on it—there must be a trail there, but Laura sees no one today—she could hear their voices, though not make out the words. The park is quiet today, but even when it's crowded, this piece of the walk seems oddly still, held in suspension, full of echoes that haven't sounded. As she walks with Helen, Laura tries to imagine how it would feel to know a truth and not need to tell it.

"My father still thinks I was lost up here all night once, when I was in high school," says Mitchell. "Or I guess he doesn't think it anymore, now that he's dead."

They are standing near the tower, making up their minds to start down. They'd climbed up the cool stone steps inside it, today, to see the view from the top, all but Dan, who paced back and forth on the lawn below them with Charlotte, who is asleep now, draped over his shoulders, her hands clasping his head, then sometimes sliding down to rest across the frames of his eyeglasses.

"You told him you were lost up *here*?" says Helen, motioning toward the gray stone tower—minimal for a tower, a sketch of a castle, built in the thirties, with just enough detail (a turret here and there) to have a hint of the romantic about it.

"Yeah. Not right here—on one of the trails. Actually, I'd been with a girl—at her house. Her parents were away—"

"You mean you'd both been hiking here—" Helen says.

"No, we hadn't even been here. I don't know what made me think of it. I just said it, when I got in, the next morning, and he wanted to know where I'd been all night. My dad was a riot about it." They have started down, and Mitchell stops to kick a pebble as he talks. "He believed me. He got all excited about it."

"And you never told him the truth?" says Laura, thinking of Mitchell's father, a genial man who'd had some job or other in a state office—he commuted to Hartford every day—and who had died suddenly of a heart attack about a year ago.

"Oh, you couldn't do that, it was such a thing with him," says Mitchell, shaking his head and laughing. "My dad loved hiking—camping—that sort of thing. Well, for years he talked about it, how I was lost here—"

"Do you do that to me, Mitchell?" says Helen, almost—but not quite—as if the question were a joke.

"Do what?"

"Lie to me."

"Oh, come on, Helen—" says Mitchell. "It wasn't exactly—" His voice has dropped a little. It usually has a slightly metallic ring, Laura realizes, but now it's softer. She notices that she is listening closely to Mitchell, almost trying to silence the sound of her feet, to hear him more clearly. She wants to remember what he says, not to react. Soon she'll be home—then she will let herself know what she thinks. "He'd sit there," says Mitchell, "with the *Connecticut Walk Book,* or a trail map. He was a scoutmaster for years, you know, even after I got too old for it. He had all that stuff down pat. All of a sudden he'd say to me, 'Now, son, I can see how you could have drifted from the Yellow Trail to the Purple Trail in the dark—but how you ended up on the White Trail I'll never know'—or something like that. Maybe it was the other way around—*I* don't remember them all." He moves closer to Helen and rests his arm for a moment on her shoulders. Then he holds out his other arm, just a little and just briefly, but Laura is suddenly afraid that he's intending to draw her in too, and she twists away, almost bumping into Dan.

"Watch it," says Dan in a low voice, looking down—Charlotte's hands are covering his glasses. "She'll wake up." And then, having spoken, he continues to talk—coming out of his thoughts—as if he's just been awakened himself. "Mitchell," he says, turning his head carefully to catch his son-in-law's eye, "are you done with that lamp? Maybe I'll come by tonight and pick it up."

It's a powerful work light, with a long cord, which Mitchell borrowed from Dan a week or so ago. The house he wants to buy has an unlit crawl space under the roof, and Dan had suggested he examine it thoroughly, and poke the roof a bit.

"You know, as a matter of fact, I'm not," says Mitchell. "It's a funny thing—I've been meaning to call that guy all week, to arrange to go through the house again—and I just haven't had a chance to do it. But I can give the light back to you. I'm sure a flashlight will do."

"No, no," says Dan quickly. "There's no hurry."

"I really must get to that," Mitchell says. "I want to take some measurements too. I've got terrific ideas about this house, Laura," he goes on, making her his special audience. "The kitchens—I'm going to put in all new fixtures. . . . One of these days you and I will have to have lunch and go through the house together. I can use some of your insight. . . ." His voice drifts off, but when Laura doesn't say anything—she's walking hard, digging her feet in, trying not to—he goes on. "I think you and I have similar taste, Laura—we're a little artistic. Helen's more the practical type—she can't see what people like us are excited about sometimes."

Laura is sure, as she starts to answer him, that she will say only one thing—but the words feel good coming out of her mouth. She can almost feel a wind rushing them along, propelling them from inside her.

"I don't think you and I have similar taste, Mitchell," she says.

"Well, I was putting it roughly—" says Mitchell.

"In fact," Laura interrupts him, "most of what you like looks ugly to me—I don't see the point of pretending. And I don't know why you're constantly—"

"Mom," says Helen. "Wait a minute!"

But Laura can't listen, though she is surprised to hear her own words, and frightened, and she sees Dan looking at her, reaching his hand out toward her, then quickly taking hold of Charlotte's ankle again.

"You know, Mitchell—you're lying to yourself about that house," Laura says, facing him, talking fast. "In fact, you're *always* lying to yourself. And Helen doesn't even want you to buy it. As a matter of fact—"

She doesn't finish the sentence; she stops, and is already sorry, but then she adds, "She told Dan."

"Mom—" cries Helen, again.

The backs of Laura's hands are tingling. For a while there is no other answer to what she has said, only the sound of their feet on the gravel. They continue down the hill, Laura a little ahead of the others. She can still hear her own voice in her mind, quick and angry. She finds herself picturing them all hurrying down, as if she were behind their group and a little above it, up the hill, or even hovering in the air. Each of them is walking apart, leaning slightly forward—as people do when they're alone. She can see their hair, and Dan's light-blue shirt with Charlotte hunched on top, Helen's loose navy T-shirt, Mitchell's broad back—it looks scared—in white. She herself is just ahead of the others, and now her mind's eye moves forward to look at herself—the tails of the plaid flannel shirt flapping as she walks, and the back of her head—she has short brown straight hair turning gray; she's narrow and athletic; forty-eight. She is moving past slim dark trees that lean over the track, and rocks, and an occasional older, larger tree. Sometimes, when the path turns, a slice of the view, all the way down, breaks into the blur of the forest. She's wearing sneakers, and one lace is untied. With each step, its ends float up and fall.

A r t   I s   L o s t

*T*here is a cup of coffee on the table, and sunlight has plucked a quivering circle from its surface and cast it onto the ceiling as a spot of light—which shifts and moves so rapidly that Deborah, watching it without thinking while talking on the phone with her father (it's his birthday), can't figure out what it is, for a moment, once it catches her attention. She takes a sip from the cup to see whether she can let the spot go and find it again, and when she puts the cup down the light reappears—elongated now—swings from side to side, and then becomes the quivering circle once more.

She loves and misses her father and mother. Her parents, both retired, live several hundred miles from the city where Deborah works as a children's librarian. Her father used to be a history teacher in a high school. When Deborah was a child, he wrote historical novels during the summers, and Deborah assumed until recently that he was still writing, and still reading American history, his specialty. Every year she bought him a history book or a historical novel for his birthday, and told her friends that her father's interests kept him young. But a few months ago, when she visited her parents, she asked him about the latest birthday book, and he said he hadn't finished it; when she examined the bookshelf, all her recent presents looked unread. It has been years since he showed her a manuscript, though when asked he says he's writing about Thomas Jefferson.

Deborah was angry about the books, though she didn't say so, and when her father's birthday came near, she put off shopping for his present. This morning—on his birthday—she finally bought a sweater, a red cardigan. It came in gray and brown too, but in the store, red seemed better. "Wake him up," she had said—but her father sounds *awake*.

"So I merely pointed out to the receptionist," he says—he's been fighting about money with his doctor—"that right on her desk were Xerox copies of *all* the correspondence she said didn't exist!" But Deborah hasn't been following.

"Did that convince them?" she hazards. The level of coffee is now too low to pick up the light, though she tips the cup from side to side, and raises it up.

"Well, I don't know," he says. "As I told you, I'm waiting to see whether the new bill has the same mistake."

"Oh, right," says Deborah, then, "I'm sorry I haven't sent you a birthday present—but I *bought* it—not a book this year."

"All right," he says.

"I'll mail it tomorrow," says Deborah. "It's a little daring." She is suddenly unsure about the red. "Promise to tell me the truth if you don't like it."

"You don't have to mail it," says her father. "You'll be here in three weeks."

"I don't want you to have to wait three weeks."

When he gives the phone to her mother, Deborah makes

her promise not to tell, and describes the red sweater. Her mother says anything at all will be fine. "You'll be here soon," she says with a little laugh of anticipation. "Did you make a reservation?"

Deborah is not just going for a visit. She has been invited to give a talk to her mother's Senior Study Group, although when the invitation arrived—a letter from the president of the group, who knew that Deborah was a librarian, and said she could speak on any topic she liked—Deborah had phoned her parents and had an argument with her mother.

"You made her write that letter," she said. "If you want me to visit you, say so. I don't need some phony invitation."

"Deborah, the president called me up and asked for your address. That's all I knew about it." Deborah didn't believe her, but she wrote to the woman and agreed, proposing to repeat a lecture, which she associates with good luck, that she'd given at a college near where she lives, a few months ago. The lecture had come about when Deborah put together an exhibit of illustrations from old children's books at her library. A professor at the college who happened to see the exhibit invited Deborah to speak, paid her, and even found money to have the illustrations photographed and slides made. It will be a pleasure to show the slides—and to see them—again.

Deborah finishes her coffee and washes the cup, the receiver balanced on her shoulder. She is restless, talking to her mother, and her hands want something to do—she sponges a countertop—but soon she and her mother get off the phone.

The Mandelbaums' living room gets the sun in the afternoon, and on the day of Deborah's talk she and her mother have time to sit there for an hour after lunch. Deborah had arrived the night before; they'd walked to the store together in the morning. Deborah's father slept late and was having his breakfast when they'd come back with the groceries. Now *he's* gone for a walk; he'll be out for several hours, and they won't see him until after the talk.

"I knew you'd want him to come," her mother says, "even if he's not a regular member, but he said no."

"No, I *don't* want him to come," says Deborah, not sure she's telling the truth. Her mother looks hurt. "I'm not an expert speaker," Deborah says. "Let's keep it casual and simple—as if I met some of your friends by chance. If Dad came, that would make it a big event."

"We do have officers and a regular program," says her mother. "We have a speaker once a month. We had a nice write-up in the paper last year."

"Of course I know that," says Deborah. Her mother is sitting on a straight chair between two windows—she says only straight chairs feel comfortable lately. The windows are divided into panes, and the sun is coming through both of them. It's a little hard to see her mother because Deborah is facing her, and facing the windows with their rectangles of light—which are repeated, as parallelograms, on the floor on either side of her.

"You'll like my slides," says Deborah, after a silence. She had found half a dozen illustrations, from books written at different times, of children with their dogs. Some are idealized and sentimental, others realistic. In her favorite, a wise collie stands guard over a sleeping baby. In the older pictures, she's noticed, the pets are often in charge, while in the modern ones the children—unisex, overalled persons, with hair hanging into their eyes—lord it over huge, foolish, adoring dogs.

"Anything at all will be *fine*," says her mother, which, Deborah recalls, is what she said about her father's birthday present when Deborah described it on the phone. Her father hasn't mentioned it. Deborah meant to mail it right away, but a week passed before she wrapped it and took it to the post office.

"Did Dad get the sweater?" she says.

"Oh," says her mother, who looks confused but quickly remembers, "the sweater—the red sweater you bought for his birthday. Of course it came. It's beautiful. He asked me to tell you."

"He asked you to tell me? Why didn't he tell me himself?"

"If he forgot," she says. "We were talking about it yesterday, the red sweater, and he said, 'If I forget to mention it, be sure to tell Deborah how much I like it.' "

"That's good," says Deborah, wishing he'd remembered. "I'm glad he didn't think it was too bright."

"No," her mother says. "It's beautiful."

Mrs. Mandelbaum goes back to the kitchen for a fruit bowl. She no longer puts a paper doily under the fruit, as she did when Deborah was a child—though it's the same bowl, amber glass with a design cut in it, and there is a single banana curved protectively around the apples, oranges, and pears, as of old.

"You need energy," her mother says, offering the bowl.

Deborah shakes her head. She's a little nervous, and she wonders what she needs now, if not fruit. She'd like her mother to tell stories, she thinks, as her friends would—they'd be stories of speeches and recitals and performances—and always (come to think of it) there would be a mistake or a mishap; but the stories would help, anyway—they'd be comical, and they wouldn't, exactly, be about *failure*.

"I bought pears early in the week," her mother says. "I left time for them to ripen. See? Bosc pears."

"My friend Cindy," says Deborah, taking an apple and holding it on her lap, "was once a page turner at a concert, and by mistake she knocked the music off the stand." Cindy, a pianist, has told her many stories. "She caught it on her foot."

"Imagine that!" says her mother.

"And another time she was playing in a chamber-music concert and when she turned the page, the next page wasn't there."

"Didn't the page turner turn the page?"

"I don't know if she *had* a page turner," Deborah says. "The point is—she had the back of the page to play, and then nothing. She says she just made up music and nobody noticed."

The doorbell rings—Deborah's mother no longer drives, and a friend has come by to give them a ride to the meeting. Later, her father will come and drive them home. Mrs. Mandelbaum hurries to the door, stepping across one of the grids of sunlight on the floor. Her face, which is heavy these days, is suddenly lit with sun and excitement as she turns to the side and smiles at Deborah. "Do you remember the talk your father gave that summer?" she says. "I have a family of celebrities."

Only one of Mr. Mandelbaum's historical novels was ever printed. At a crossword-puzzle tournament he entered when Deborah was ten or eleven, he met a man who ran a small press somewhere in upstate New York called Iron Kettle Books. The man offered to publish Mr. Mandelbaum's most recent novel, *Across the Lake in Darkness,* which was about Ethan Allen and the Green Mountain Boys.

Deborah never found her father's book in a bookstore, though she looked, but when it came out it was reviewed in the newsletter of a historical society somewhere near the press, and thus came into the hands of a woman who wrote to her father, care of the press. She owned a summer cottage—she called it a "camp"—somewhere on the New York side of Lake Champlain, which, she said, she was lending him for the month of

August of that year. She said he had a "rare talent." Deborah's mother said, "It's some kind of trick," but her father wrote back and said they'd come, and the woman sent directions. She had also arranged for Mr. Mandelbaum to give a talk, followed by a reception, to the historical society, or maybe it was the literary society, of the town where she lived—which was rather far from the cottage, Deborah remembers. Maybe it was Glens Falls.

The cottage was a few feet from the shore of the lake, with a long wooden dock out into the water. It was always cold there, and Deborah's parents said it was sad that she couldn't swim very much, but Deborah was happy to read instead. Her bedroom had a low, slanting ceiling, and wallpaper—the walls at home were painted—that covered the ceiling too. It depicted old-fashioned children in profile, girls and boys in alternating rows over each other's heads. The girls were in sunbonnets, each looking ahead of her at the back of the next girl, so their faces didn't show. The boys were raising sticks to push tall hoops, except that in one place, near the door, the sticks pushed nothing, and all the hoops were high over the heads of all the boys, like big balloons escaping. Deborah liked the girls' long dresses—there were two kinds, pink and blue—and she liked to think that when the cottage had been built and the wallpaper hung the styles were in fashion, which wasn't true, of course.

Deborah's father still likes talking about the surprise of the woman's letter—especially to people who have just said that nothing interesting is going to turn up, not for *them*. "You have no idea who may be sitting down to write you a letter at this very moment," her father says. He tells them about the cottage, and the talk, and how afterward, at the reception, he was given three kinds of cake to try, one after another.

* * *

The Senior Study Group meets in the basement of a church, in a large room filled with rows of folding chairs. Windows run along one wall, up high, and there are no drapes or shades; coming in with her bravely smiling mother, Deborah wonders about showing her slides. She'd requested a slide projector and a screen when she wrote to the president, but she doesn't see them. In the room are a tall old man talking in a loud, deep voice, and four or five women, two of them arranging plates of cookies on a table. A woman comes over to Deborah and her mother; she begins to nod and smile when she is ten feet away. "You told me about your daughter," she says gently to Deborah's mother. "Is this your daughter?" She is tiny, with white hair in a plain cut.

"This is Mrs. Green," Deborah's mother tells Deborah.

"Please call me Leah," says Mrs. Green. "We are both biblical, Deborah and Leah. It's good of you to come." She almost bows, and Deborah finds herself almost bowing back.

"Deborah is today's speaker," says her mother. "Don't you remember?"

"Oh, Edith, I didn't!" says Leah. "But I'm always in a fog. Don't go by me." She turns to Deborah. "And what is your subject?"

Deborah says she is going to talk about the history of illustrations in children's books.

"Art is the best subject," says Leah.

"Are you an artist?" Deborah asks.

"Do not dignify my feeble efforts—" Leah begins, laughing, but Deborah's mother interrupts.

"Last year we had a show, in this very room, of Leah's oil paintings."

"Watercolors," says Leah mournfully.

There is a lectern in one corner of the room, and the president of the study group, Celeste Carpenter, is pushing it toward the front, scraping it across the wooden floor. Deborah and her mother hurry to help her, but she has reached the front of the room and is trying to position the lectern more precisely when they catch up to her and Deborah is introduced.

"Oh, *Deborah*," says Mrs. Carpenter, a tall, vague woman who seems to need to call her arms and legs to order, like wandering children, before she can focus her pale blue eyes on Deborah. "Did you come to get a preview?" she says curiously.

"Deborah is today's speaker, of course," her mother says.

"Next month," says Celeste quickly, her arms and legs in distracted motion again. "Remember? Next month. Today's speaker is Brian Johnson. I can't find the ice-water pitcher."

"Wait a minute," says Deborah gently—she knows she hasn't made a mistake, but she can see that Mrs. Carpenter is being as clearheaded as she *can* be.

Her mother, however, is outraged. "I never *heard* of any Brian Johnson!" she says.

"The radio personality?" says Celeste. "He has that call-in show at night. We were lucky to get him—but what did I do? Is *he* coming next month?" She pulls a battered datebook from her purse, and she and Deborah's mother turn the pages, head to head.

"Come on, Celeste," says Deborah's mother. "You're not really looking!"

"Wait, wait—I do have a system," says Celeste, but a man in his thirties approaches them. He is bright-faced, and carries a large, hard attaché case.

"Brian Johnson," he says happily, shaking their hands one after another. "Brian Johnson."

"I appeal to *you*," says Deborah's mother immediately. She

tells him the story. "You come next month," she says. "Deborah can't. The plane fare! And she had to take off from work."

"I think Mr. Johnson can't make it next month," says Celeste.

Deborah herself is more fascinated than angry, and is thinking of withdrawing her claim, but Brian Johnson says, "Surely we can *share* the podium," and that's how they settle it, eventually. Celeste cheers up after a while and says the afternoon will be better than she expected. The two of them have something in common, she says.

The day Deborah's father gave his talk to the literary society, all those years ago, Deborah went along with her parents to hear him. She was the only child present. Her father talked comfortably about Ethan Allen, as if the audience were made up of his own history students. He explained that no one knew exactly what Ethan Allen and the other historical personages had said, so he had invented speeches for them. Deborah thought that was obvious, and the members of the society would think her father was talking down to them, but they didn't mind, and later someone asked how historians knew what Ethan Allen had said, and her father had to explain again.

After the talk, ladies brought her father coffee with milk and sugar, the way he liked it, and a piece of layer cake. They stood near him and asked him questions, and the lady who had arranged it all, the owner of the cottage, acted as if she were in charge and stood nearest of all, keeping an eye on anyone who spoke to him. Deborah and her mother had to look after themselves. To give herself something to do, Deborah went over to the refreshment table, where a half-circle of paper cups full of Hawaiian Punch stood behind a plate of cupcakes. The cupcakes had white icing and shredded coconut on top, and when she reached over them and took a cup of punch, she spilled it right on the cupcakes. Immediately, ten arms, each led by a hand holding a folded white paper napkin, reached from every direction around her—one, in fact, came down over her shoulder, grazing her chest—at the dark pink puddles on the paper plate and on the white paper tablecloth. The arms hemmed her in while the napkins patted up the spilled punch. Deborah stood helplessly, looking around for her mother.

"Children, children!" said a woman's light voice behind her. "Art is lost on children."

"Well, it's nothing to make such a fuss about," said Deborah's mother, but Deborah hadn't been offended, though she knew she wasn't a clumsy child, and that art wasn't lost on her—whether the woman meant the art of sprinkling shredded coconut or her father's literary art. The woman's voice was a little exasperated—but mostly it was humorous, nothing like her parents' nervous voices, and all at once Deborah had fallen in love with her. She was sure the woman had six rowdy children—in sunbonnets, like the girls on the wallpaper, possibly with hoops—and she wanted to go live among them and be cheerfully scolded when they all fell out of the hayloft or into the pond with the turtles. It was amusement in the face of disorder that she'd glimpsed, and though her mother pulled her away (she was the one who minded about the spilled punch, of course) and Deborah didn't get a piece of cake, she still— even now, sitting on her folding chair next to Brian Johnson, while Mrs. Carpenter opens the meeting of the Senior Study Group—finds solace in the memory.

"Books!" Celeste Carpenter explains to the audience, ten or twelve people—scattered, as if each has a stubborn private theory about where to sit at lectures. "We had a little mix-up here," she says. "But Deborah—Edith Mandelbaum's daughter—is a *librarian*. And you certainly know Brian Johnson, but you may not know something he told me on the phone. He's writing a book! About the Beatles, I think."

Brian Johnson nods.

"And so," Mrs. Carpenter concludes, both arms spread wide, "today's subject is 'Books' "—which means it's time for Deborah to speak. She stands up. Someone has gone to look for the slide projector, not that the room is dark enough. She can't show her slides and she doesn't know how to discuss "Books." But there is Leah in the first row, over to the side, gazing at her, her straight white hair standing out in the sunlight that's coming through the windows. Deborah's mother is also in the first row, at the other side, turning her purse over and over in her lap. Deborah begins. She sounds boring to herself at first, trying to adapt her original lecture, but after a while she finds new things to say, and talks in a livelier voice. Then the slide projector turns up, and Deborah gets excited, talking about the picture of the collie, who stands out faintly on the tan wall behind her, swollen slightly over a strip of molding. Everyone laughs because she is so enthusiastic, but then Mrs. Carpenter asks her to stop—it's Brian's turn. Deborah is disappointed, but she's already imagining the account of this day she'll give her friends back home, and she tells herself that being interrupted will just be another good bit. She sits down amid applause.

Brian Johnson has taken the afternoon's new topic seriously. Before Deborah spoke, she'd seen the outline he was studying—a real outline, with Roman numerals, capital letters, Arabic numbers, and small letters. He was going to talk about "The Life of a Talk-Show Host," and when Deborah peered over his shoulder he was looking over the second page, which

began, "III. Guest Fails to Show Up. A. Weather B. Sickness."
It seems, though, that Brian has penciled in a new speech—on
books, or on the subject of his own book, if there really is a
book; that is, he talks about the Beatles—about whom Deborah's mother, for one, probably knows only that they sang and
had long hair. Deborah herself was in her teens when the Beatles became popular, and at first was too intellectual to listen
to them much, but in college a boyfriend taught her to take
them seriously, and she has two of their albums at home, *Rubber Soul* and *Sgt. Pepper*. But Brian, who is flushed with pleasure at the chance to talk about the Beatles, obviously knows
all about them. "Of course George did the lyrics on that one,"
he says—he talks rapidly, with little laughs, "which was surprising, considering—well, a lot of things going on that year,
the management stuff, *of course,* and how things were with the
previous album. . . ." At last he mentions "Yellow Submarine,"
and the old man Deborah noticed before begins to sing it—as
if he'd finally, delightedly, grasped what was going on.

After a while, Brian too is interrupted. Celeste says it's now
the Discussion Period, and someone asks Brian whether rock
music is bad for young people; next the audience discusses
loud radios at the beach. Everyone is in favor of a proposed
ordinance to ban boom boxes except one woman, who timidly
mentions the First Amendment, but is shouted down.

Now Deborah looks up; her father has come into the room,
and is standing behind the last row of folding chairs. He seems
troubled. Deborah's father still looks like a high-school teacher
to her—gray-haired, serious, not very big—and, somehow,
wherever he is always starts to look like a high school. He
glances about as if he's going to hand out detentions or remind
people that he takes off for spelling, and fastens his gaze on a
woman near the front who is speaking. "Maybe I'm crazy—but

I like the Beatles," she says. She wiggles her hips in her chair, flutters her fingers, and sings, "Will you still feed me—when I'm sixty-four?" Then she laughs apologetically, and Brian and Deborah applaud and smile at each other.

Deborah's father, however, steps forward, leaning on the back of a folding chair. "Wait a minute," he says, mildly at first, but with some intensity. Everyone in the audience turns around to look at him. "Wait just a minute. There's something amiss here. I didn't come today"—his voice becomes louder, and angry, and scornful—"to hear about the *Beatles*! I thought you people cared about *art—that's* what I came to hear about. Art in *books—*" Deborah realizes that he is trying to rescue her—not that she wants to be rescued—but he can't quite remember the subject of her talk. Then he finishes grimly, "Art in *library books*!"

There is silence for quite a while, but then Deborah hears Leah's measured voice. "When I was a child," she begins, "I had no books but library books. I went to the library—well, it might have been every day. You were allowed to take out one book, and so I'd choose carefully, and then I'd walk home, reading it." She demonstrates, holding an imaginary book up to her face and staring at it. "The next day, I'd borrow another book. Except for the fairy-tale books. They took two days, three days. . . ."

"*The Blue Fairy Book*," someone says dreamily. "*The Violet Fairy Book . . .*"

There is a pause, and another woman says, "In my library— my childhood library—a big staircase led to the children's room. There was a fireplace with built-in seats around it. I'd go on a Friday, after school. Maybe it would be snowing outside, or raining. I'd sit in a corner of the seats and read."

Then Deborah's mother speaks. She recalls a weekly story hour when she was a girl, and how one day the designated room was locked, and the librarian read to the children in a hallway, sitting on the floor. "She couldn't disappoint us," Edith Mandelbaum says, turning a little and gesturing. Deborah has never heard her tell that story before. "She was young and blond. I remember her reading a picture book, *Johnny Crow's Garden.*"

"I remember that book!" says Brian. He leans forward and speaks more slowly than he did before, easily, as if they were all in a living room, not a public place. "My mother read it to me."

Then he sits back, as if at rest, and everyone else seems to sit back, all at once, Deborah too, as if there has been a rescue—of sorts—after all. It is the end of the Discussion Period, and while they all stand near the refreshment table, several people say thank-you to Deborah. "Aren't you glad you're a librarian?" says Leah. "Sixty years from now, old ladies will talk about *you.*" Deborah drinks a cup of coffee and eats a cookie, and then she and her parents say good-bye to everyone, and go outside, and get into the car.

Deborah's mother is angry with Celeste Carpenter for interrupting Deborah, and for the mix-up, and her father is upset that anyone might consider the Beatles or the host of a call-in show the proper subjects of a study group. "You see, Edith," he says, as they drive home—the sun is going down, and there's a warm light over everything—"that's why I don't belong. You people don't study, you talk about trash. A study group should deal with literature, classical music—"

"We do, we do," Deborah's mother says impatiently. "Why do you think we invited Deborah? This was an exception."

"The Beatles aren't trash," says Deborah. She's tired, and she would rather be with people who'd like hearing about Brian's outline and her impressions of Celeste—though, all in all, she's glad she delivered her talk.

Then her father says, "Deborah! In all this excitement I almost forgot—what do you think arrived? Your sweater. The sweater you sent me for my birthday."

"That's all right," she says. "Mother told me it came."

She is sitting in the back seat, and he glances swiftly over his shoulder at her. "Mother told you?" he says. "How could she tell you? She doesn't know. It came this afternoon, just as I was leaving to pick you up. I almost missed the delivery, and then I'd have had to go to the post office. See? You wasted the postage. You could have brought it with you."

She can't see her mother's face. "Mother," she says, "why did you lie to me? Why did you tell me it came?"

But her mother is proud that she lied. She says she was doing Deborah a favor. If she had told the truth, she says, Deborah would have been worried about the present all afternoon, afraid it had been lost in the mail. "It would have affected your concentration," she says. "I bet you didn't insure it."

"It wasn't that kind of afternoon," says Deborah. "It wasn't that kind of present."

"You have no reason to be angry, Deborah," says her father. "That was impressive of Mother—she had to think fast. And, really, it was hardly even a lie." He pauses and goes on. "She *had* to do it. It was like touching up a photograph—art, not lying."

"But people *shouldn't* touch up photographs," says Deborah from the back seat. "She *didn't* have to." Then, "What do you know about art?" Art is lost to her father, it seems to her now, or never did matter—and her mother's art, if that's what it is, is lost on her. But she sees that they don't understand her.

From the middle of the back seat, she looks at the tops of their heads against the late-afternoon sky. Both of them have gray hair; it seems darker than it really is, inside the car. Her mother's is thick and evenly waved, but her father's is thin and straight, combed from left to right across the back of his head. As her father parks the car near their house, Deborah pictures herself sitting forward and cupping her hands on their two heads, above the high back of their seats—shaking them, or fondling their hair, or maybe knocking their heads together. The moment passes and they are all out of the car, but Deborah's mother's collar is standing up, and her father has a bit of lint on his shoulder, so their daughter can pat and ruffle the two of them, a little, after all.

. . . .

Painting Day

*F*ranny and her friend Meg are sitting on the floor of Meg's newly rented, empty apartment, which they are painting today, eating baked potatoes with broccoli and cheese sauce from Wendy's. Franny has just come from buying new paint rollers. On the way back, she had stopped to pick up lunch for both of them, and also for Stephanie and Max—her daughter and Meg's son. She'd been driving Meg's car because Stephanie was using hers. Stephanie's sixteen, and she's taking care of Max, who is two. They've gone to Brooksvale Park, several miles away, to look at the farm animals there—two cows, a pig (Max's favorite), innumerable rabbits. . . . . It keeps raining, on and off, so they won't be gone for long. This is the first time Stephanie has driven with a child in the car.

Franny remembers to return Meg's keys and Meg reminds Franny to keep track of what she owes her. Franny nods, though she is already uncertain of the amount. She has begun to worry a little about Stephanie and Max. She'd half expected they would be back before her.

Meg gathers up the wrappings from their lunch, stuffs them into a bag of trash, and stacks the two remaining lunches at the back corner of the kitchen counter where they won't be knocked off by trays and rollers and cans of paint. They are going to paint Max's room next. Franny puts on a paint-spattered shirt. She rolls up the sleeves, follows Meg into Max's room, which they'd scraped and swept before lunch, and offers to do the woodwork.

"You'd better," says Meg. "I'd botch it up." She pours some paint—off-white—into a tray, dips her roller, and begins to sweep it rapidly, in slightly curved, uneven swaths, over the center of the largest open section of wall. Franny pries open another can of paint, mixes it, and starts to work on the ridged window frame. She glances out the window. It's raining steadily now. She's not sure it's a good idea to paint on a rainy day.

"I've been needing to tell you something since Thursday," Meg says. It's Saturday. "I'm mad at Larry." Larry is a second-grade teacher whom Meg has been seeing for several months. She'd been married to a man named Ken, but they are divorced.

"What did he do?"

"I went to his house on Thursday, right after work," Meg says. "Ken was taking care of Max." She stops to sop up more paint on her roller, driving it up and down in the tray a few times. "Anyway, I went straight to Larry's place, and—well, we went straight to bed. After we made love we both fell asleep. I don't know what time it was—I woke up because the doorbell was ringing. There we were—I thought it must be the paper boy or something, but Larry opened his eyes and stared at me. Did you ever see him without his glasses?"

"No," says Franny.

"Well, he looks very innocent, and a little wild, like a religious fanatic. His eyes are so *blue.* Anyway, he said, 'I just remembered I invited my parents to dinner.' "

Franny, kneeling to paint the windowsill, turns around and sits back on her heels. "He didn't!"

"He did."

"That's awful. Was it terribly embarrassing?"

"Well, not really. We got dressed and let them in—they're very nice. It worked out. But I was angry with him. Is that unreasonable of me? He says he just forgot." Meg stops painting and sits down on the floor. "Do you think he secretly hates me and he did it on purpose to humiliate me?"

"I don't think so."

"Neither do I," says Meg, "though of course that's what I said."

"Was he sorry?"

"He was apology personified," says Meg, getting up again. "You'd think it wouldn't bother me. I mean, after Ken. Larry's *decent.*"

"I don't know," says Franny. "Jack is decent, but there are times you need them to be decent and *not* to forget." Jack is Franny's husband. Franny, who has gone back to painting, turns around again. "Remember when Stephanie was sick, the way he screwed up all the *little* things? I knew it was because he was scared, but that didn't always help."

"I remember," says Meg. Stephanie, after a suicide attempt that no one had foreseen or could explain, had spent three months in a psychiatric hospital, ending a year and a half ago. Sometimes it seems to Franny that it can't have been that long ago, and at other times as if it happened years and years earlier, or in another life. Today it is in her mind, possibly because Stephanie is driving, and caring for Max.

Meg crouches to dip her roller again. "I'm not *really* mad at him," she says. "But I couldn't wait to tell you." She laughs. Then she says over her shoulder, "But where *is* Stephanie? Wouldn't you think she'd be tired of baby-sitting by now?"

"What bothers me," says Franny, her anxieties released by the question, "is that your phone isn't hooked up yet."

"That's reassuring too, though," says Meg. "If she ran out of gas or something like that—you know, just a delay—she'd have to call your house for help, and we wouldn't know about it."

"There's plenty of gas," says Franny. She makes herself continue painting and they are silent for a while. Franny listens to the sound of Meg's roller, which hits the wall every few seconds with a little more force than is necessary. Meg won't be bothered to put masking tape around windows when she paints window frames, so she can't be allowed to do woodwork.

"Don't you hate the way your mind goes, when something like this happens?" Meg says finally. She turns around to look at Franny again. One lock of Meg's hair, which is brown, is always falling into her eyes. Now specks of white paint make it look as if it's starting to go gray. Franny's hair is short, so she need not brush it aside all the time—but it really *is* getting gray. Meg goes on, "You know, I've just been imagining Max's funeral."

"You too?" says Franny. "I thought you had sense. I haven't been able to choose, myself—Steffie's funeral, Max's funeral, a *double* funeral . . ." There is no one but Meg with whom she could have this conversation. Her voice has been light but when Meg doesn't say anything for a moment she speaks again, and lets it become more serious. "Meg, I shouldn't have let her take Max. What if she's still sick, really? What if she did something crazy?"

Meg comes over to her and puts one hand—the one not

holding the roller—on Franny's shoulder. "She didn't do any-thing crazy," she says.

Larry and Stephanie are behaving like a team—the team everyone has been waiting for—and they point out that if all four of them paint the kitchen together it will be done in no time. They say it's astonishing how long it took Franny and Meg to paint the bedroom. Stephanie and Max had arrived just as Larry turned up, offering to help, and just as Franny hurried down the street toward a public phone—she'd decided to call Jack, finally. Halfway to the corner she realized that a shout behind her was meant for her—"One, two, three—Mom!" From the sound of it, they were all yelling, and it was about their third try. She'd turned and walked back to them. They were waving and laughing. Stephanie, chunky in a big square jacket made out of some kind of heavy gray cotton, looked solid and safe, with something in each hand—Max on one side of her, and—what was that?—his car seat on the other. Larry looked tall, wild-haired, and narrow beside her, wiping the rain off his glasses with his thumbs. Franny was proud of the way Ste-phanie kept hold of Max's hand, then made sure Franny was watching him when she went to put the car seat into the back seat of Meg's car, but she was angry and almost cried, and she still feels bad, she realizes now, as she sits on the kitchen floor looking at woodwork again—she's angry at having been fright-ened, she's unsettled. Stephanie had simply forgotten she'd said she'd be right back, and forgotten the lunch her mother was buying for her. It was raining, she pointed out, so she and Max couldn't hang around in the park. So she had taken him home to their house—"Where else would I be?"—and fed him a grilled cheese sandwich. She finally came back when his diaper leaked through and his pants were wet. She didn't have a change of diapers.

Now Max, in his shirt and fresh diaper but no pants, is sitting on the floor with a blue bandanna that belongs to Meg tied around his head, pirate style, eating cold french fries from Wendy's. Larry is painting the kitchen ceiling with a roller that has a long pole fitted to the end of its handle, and Stephanie is sitting cross-legged on the counter, painting the wall above it with a brush. Meg has left—she's driven over to her old apartment for clean pants for Max, who will be picked up soon. Ken is taking him to his house.

"Want hat," Max had said, as Meg bent to tell him she'd be right back, wearing the bandanna around her hair. She took it off and put it on Max's head. Now Franny sees that Max has finished his french fries and is starting to look troubled.

"Max, do you want to see how you look? You have a funny hat on," she reminds him.

"Want see." She carries him into the bathroom and holds him up so he can look at himself in the mirror over the basin. Max laughs. He pulls the bandanna off and reaches up to lay it across the top of Franny's head. She puts him down and ties it under her own chin like a babushka. Max laughs at that too, and they go back to the kitchen.

Stephanie has put the stepladder, which they'd brought this morning—the aluminum folding kind with three steps—on top of the counter. Now she hoists herself back up to the counter, climbs the stepladder, and scrambles belly-first onto the top of a wooden cupboard on the wall. "Is this thing going to hold my weight?" she asks.

"What if the answer is no?" says Franny, more sharply than she expects. "Do you plan to put the wall back together again?"

Stephanie doesn't answer. She holds still for a moment, and

then she starts moving naturally again. The cabinet doesn't fall down. "Yuck," she says. "It's filthy up here. Mom, hand me my brush and the paint, would you?"

"Up!" says Max, stretching his arms and straining toward the top of the counter.

"Shall I give you something to clean the cabinet with?" says Franny.

"I'll do it later," Stephanie says. Franny doesn't want to argue with her, and says nothing. Stephanie begins to paint the wall above the cabinet, and Franny sets the ladder back down on the floor so she can do something for Max, who is still calling "Up!" and is growing impatient. She sits him on top of the ladder, holding him by his waist, and then, at his insistence, holds his hand so that he can climb down the steps and back up, over and over. His socks have disappeared into his sneakers, and Franny leans over to pull them out. They're a little damp.

"When I was in the hospital last year," says Stephanie thoughtfully, after a few minutes, "there was this one nurse who used to say people were bouncing off the ceiling. I always thought that was weird, that you're supposed to say 'bouncing off the walls.' Well, right now I'm bouncing off the ceiling." Stephanie can just sit comfortably, there on top of the cupboard, without bumping her head. She reaches up and touches the ceiling.

"What were you in the hospital for?" says Larry.

"I was in the looney bin," says Stephanie. Franny stops herself from speaking.

"Oh," says Larry. "Psychiatric. That must have been a bummer." He doesn't seem embarrassed, as far as Franny can tell.

"It was," says Stephanie. "I tried to do myself in."

Franny is helping Max up and down the stairs of the stepladder. Her irritation with Stephanie has been replaced by a strange excitement—Stephanie has never talked this way in her presence. She feels as if she mustn't move abruptly, or say anything—as if she'd become aware of deer grazing behind her in a meadow.

Larry has brought his roller down and laid it for a moment in the tray of paint, and is shaking out his long, thin arm. A fine spray of white paint has speckled his face, his hair and his glasses. "That's *really* a bummer," he says.

"Well, it was very complex, actually," says Stephanie, turning from the wall to face him. But the doorbell rings.

Franny takes Max under his arms and sets him on the floor. Then she goes downstairs to see who's there. Stephanie has stopped talking. It's Ken at the door, peering up uncertainly through the glass pane in an inner door at the foot of the stairs.

"Hi," says Franny, opening it. "This is the right place."

"I wasn't sure I remembered the number," says Ken.

"Meg's not here," says Franny, as he follows her back up the stairs. "But she'll be right back. She went to the old apartment to get clean pants for Max." She knows it isn't right to be annoyed with him for interrupting Stephanie, but she is.

"Hi, Stephanie," says Ken, and "Nice to see you," with a quick nod, to Larry—they've met, Franny recalls. Ken looks clean and civilized compared to them, in a jacket and white shirt. "I don't need to see Meg," he says. "I'll just take the baby."

"But he's not wearing any pants," says Franny. "Meg went to get some."

"I think I have some of his things at my place," says Ken. "And the car's right outside."

"I think it would be better if you'd wait," Franny says. She sits down on the floor and picks up her paintbrush.

"Well, you're probably right," says Ken, "but this is when I *said* I'd come. Couldn't she have gotten things ready in time? Look, tell her I'm sorry, but I'm meeting some people at my apartment." He picks up Max. "Wanna go ride in Daddy's car?"

"Go see pig," says Max.

"See what?" says Ken. "What pig?"

"At Brooksvale Park," says Stephanie. "I took him this morning."

"Wait a minute," says Franny. "The *car seat*. It's in Meg's car." Meg is always careful about transferring it.

"Oh. Well—I'll just use the seat belt," says Ken. He reaches for Max's jacket, which is lying on top of the old newspapers. "I'll let myself out," he says. "Thanks. Come on, Maxy." And he goes. The others are all silent as his footsteps go downstairs, sounding heavy because Max is on his arm. Max is still talking about the pig. Then they hear the door close.

"Meg's not going to like that," says Larry.

"I know," says Franny. "But I didn't know what to do."

"Neither did I," Larry says. "I felt like kind of a sensitive figure in that scene, somehow."

"I bet there *aren't* any people at his house," says Stephanie from the top of the cabinet.

Meg lets herself in a few minutes later, carrying an old grocery bag and with a pair of overalls and Max's raincoat over her arm. "I brought tea," she says. "I knew you'd want coffee, Larry, but I didn't know about you, Steff. What are you doing up there? Are you a caffeine adult?" She puts the bag down on the counter. "Where's Max?"

"Tea is fine," says Stephanie. Franny has never seen her daughter drink tea.

"Well, the thing is—" Franny says, "Ken came and took him."

"Without pants, in the rain?" says Meg. "Oh, God, he's so awful. He wouldn't wait, huh?"

"I did try," says Franny. "He said he was sorry."

"She really did try, baby," says Larry, putting his arm around Meg, who leans against him for a second and moves away. "He did *not* want to hang around here."

"And without the car seat," says Meg. "I can't stand it." She takes off her coat, takes a kettle from the bag, and fills it at the sink. Franny goes back to painting woodwork, but Meg perches on the top of the stepladder, watching the kettle on the stove. She doesn't rouse herself until steam comes out. Then she makes three cups of tea and one of coffee. "How come you're wearing my scarf like that?" she says to Franny.

"I forgot it," says Franny, taking it off. "I did it to amuse Max."

"Was he upset?"

"No, he was fine."

"He didn't mind being hauled off without any pants?"

"He didn't care," says Franny. "Don't worry about him."

"I'm not," says Meg.

"I *knew* I was about to say something," says Stephanie, all of a sudden. She is still sitting on the top of the cupboard, now sipping tea, her sturdy legs, in baggy khaki pants—paint-splattered—dangling over the side. Her lavender running shoes have damp crescents in front, Franny sees. Her feet seem large.

"I was going to tell Larry how come I tried to do myself in," says Stephanie. "I knew there was something." Larry looks over at Franny.

"Mom knows all about why I did it," says Stephanie, to Franny's surprise. "Basically, it was death. Somebody at school died."

"But you hardly *knew* her—" says Franny, interrupting before she knows what she's doing.

"I know. It was the idea of it," says Stephanie. "She had cancer. I'd never really *thought* about death. Then all at once—my great-grandmother died . . ." She ticks them off on her fingers. "And Sharon—that was the girl at school—and a man on our street, and then Ginger died."

"Who was Ginger?" says Larry.

"Our dog," says Franny. "Steffie, I never knew that was important—I mean *that* important."

"It was the idea of it," says Stephanie again.

"I had a fight with Ken about Ginger," says Meg. "I was pregnant then."

"It was after the ice storm, Larry," says Franny. "About two years ago—March, I think. Remember?"

"I remember," says Larry. "There were a lot of trees down. They closed the schools."

"We had no electricity or heat for three days," says Franny. She finds she likes telling Larry about what happened, though she suspects she should let Stephanie tell. "Ginger was sixteen, although she wasn't the kind of dog that usually lives that long. She was more or less a shepherd."

"A collie, Mom," says Stephanie.

"Well, a large dog," says Franny. "She'd had two strokes. She was deaf and blind."

"She wasn't *completely* blind," says Stephanie. "That's why she minded when the lights went out."

"Anyway, we had no lights, and she kept bumping into things," says Franny, "and it was as if she just gave up. First she got diarrhea—and I didn't even have hot water. Then the diarrhea went away and she just lay there." Franny has settled back on the floor, cross-legged, to talk. She's put down her brush. "We were all wretched," she says. "Using candles—all that. Meg was pregnant. Some things are a lot harder when you're pregnant. So finally we decided to go to the movies. *Broadway Danny Rose* was playing in Orange—they had power out there. Meg and I went, and my kids, but Jack stayed home with the dog. And Ken was boycotting us."

"Because of Ginger," says Meg. "Franny and I decided that if we all got together that night it would be a little better, but then Ken wouldn't go. He said he didn't want to *see* the dog."

"She was lying in the living room," says Franny. "You couldn't entirely blame Ken. She was on the rug, with blankets. We had to have the rug cleaned later."

"He said, 'I'm not going to watch something die,'" says Meg. "So I went over to Franny's by myself, and then we decided to go to the movies." Abruptly, Meg stops talking and starts to cry. She cries hard, and Larry puts his roller down and walks over and puts his arms around her. "This is so dumb," Meg says. "I *asked* Ken to take him today, so I could pack and all. But I miss him. Oh, you *guys*—"

"You didn't get to say good-bye," says Franny. "You like to kiss his nose and so forth."

"I need time away from him," says Meg. She blows her nose. "But it's hard. And he was gone all morning today."

"Oh," says Stephanie, sounding surprised. "I should have brought him back. I didn't know."

"It doesn't matter," says Meg. "I'm just missing him. And no car seat. It's frightening."

"*Everything's* frightening," says Stephanie—then, as Franny turns toward her quickly, "no, Mom, I don't mean that. But in a *way*. In a way, everything's frightening." She gestures widely from the top of the cabinet. "Old people die—even *kids* die. I was frightened, driving him, even *with* the car seat." Then she pauses, and her shoulders settle a little. "But it was all right." Stephanie's face looks to her mother as if, from her vantage point up near the ceiling, she can see farther than before—and Franny feels different too, like the last hiker in a line, discerning a new relief up ahead.

"Anyway," Stephanie goes on, looking over to Larry, "when we got back from the movies, Ginger had died. She had *just* died."

"*Oh,*" says Larry. "Poor old Ginger." He has finished painting the ceiling, except for the edges and the part right around the light fixture, and now he walks back to where his roller is, and unscrews the pole. "Last year, in my class," he says, "a kid came in crying because his cat died. So I held a memorial service. Well, after that, every couple of days there was another *dead pet*—birds, lizards, you name it. Sometimes they'd actually bring in the corpse—the smaller pets—wrapped in a tissue—and I'd have to hold a *burial,* yet."

Stephanie laughs from the top of the cabinet.

"Finally I began to suspect foul play," Larry says. "Just for the sake of the funerals."

"Well, I wish we'd had you around when Ginger died," says Franny.

"I have a pretty good all-purpose eulogy," says Larry. He's standing at the sink washing his roller. Meg goes back to painting the walls. None of them says anything for a while.

"Mom," Stephanie says, then, "I'm done. Help me come down." Franny goes over to the cabinet and braces herself against the counter beneath it. Stephanie is now facing out into the room. She reaches down and takes Franny's arms at the elbows, and

Franny reaches up and holds her at the waist with both hands. Stephanie's middle feels solid and hard. Franny steps back as her big girl drops herself off the cabinet, her shirt front pressing into Franny's face for a moment. Then Stephanie lands heavily against her and finds her feet, while Franny takes two more quick steps backward—but doesn't lose her balance.

. . . .

The Colorful Alphabet

Joseph, my husband, used to be married to someone else—her name was Susan. As far as I know he doesn't think about her, but sometimes it feels as if he's gone into a room at the back of his head where I've never been, or else he seems to stand in a corridor in his mind, looking toward that room, or through it and through a window at the back—maybe at part of a sycamore tree, just outside, or chimneys in a town I don't know— and when that happens, I think, "Susan." I began having that thought when I first knew him, but even then, I don't believe that by "Susan" I meant his ex-wife herself. Joseph and I have been married for eighteen years, and he was married to Susan (a dancer in Santa Fe when he last heard from her, years ago; I never met her) for only two, so it isn't Susan herself at all I'm talking about—and then in a way it is.

Last summer Joseph and I rented a cabin in New Hampshire for two weeks in August. We were glad to be going on vacation—we'd been busy in July. I teach English at a community college in Boston, where we live, and I taught one course in summer school, and looked after our kids, though Tim was fifteen and Nicki was nine, and often they looked after themselves. Joseph was busier than I. He's a hospital administrator, but he also has a law degree, and last summer he was teaching health law to paralegals—at a different college—on top of his full-time job. The course ended with a final exam three days before we went to New Hampshire, so Joseph had to read his exam papers and figure out grades in a hurry, which infuriated him. "I don't know why you people put up with this stuff," he'd say, meaning teachers, apparently, and all the schedules and calendars of academic life.

At eight in the evening the night before we left, he still couldn't get started—he kept gathering his papers together and setting off for another part of the house. Finally I suggested that we go to my office. I wanted to go with him, though of course there was plenty to do at home. Before we had children, we occasionally used to work together at night in one of our offices, maybe stopping for ice cream on our way home.

We drove to the college where I teach, and Joseph settled down at my officemate's desk, his blue books spread out in front of him. Joseph always wears long-sleeved shirts, even in summer, usually white ones. His sleeves were rolled up—he rolls them carefully, so they stay that way—and he put his elbows on the desk in front of him. He has big hands and a big round head, which he supported with his hands as he read, as if the words going in made it heavier.

As for me, I'd turned in grades two days earlier, but I'd been writing a committee report that ought to have been finished by then—my department was recommending a change in the college English requirement—and so I sat down at my own desk and started looking over my notes.

"I like the way this place smells," I said, after a little, trying to decide why I didn't mind being there. It's an ugly building. "Is it chalk? It smells as if the life of the mind goes on here." The window was open and the air was a little stale but not too hot. I took my feet out of my sandals and set them on the cool tiled floor.

"I don't smell anything," said Joseph. Then I heard the elevator creak and steps coming down the corridor, and a colleague of mine, Gordon Raymond, leaned into the doorway.

"Irene," he said, "you're writing your fall syllabus!"

"I'm not *that* compulsive," I said. I explained about Joseph's grades and the cabin in New Hampshire. Gordon and Joseph had met a few times at department parties. Gordon said he hadn't yet turned in his own summer-school grades and the registrar was after him with a meat cleaver, and Joseph put down his blue book. Gordon was carrying a worn khaki knapsack that looked as if it might have come from the L. L. Bean catalog, and he leaned against my door and swung the knapsack, whacking it affectionately, not too hard, on the file cabinet next to him. The bag had a tolerated—or tolerant—look about it, as if Gordon and it had put up with each other for a long time.

"How the hell do you spell *separate*?" said Joseph, picking up a paper again.

"*A*," I said. Gordon was spelling the whole word.

"These kids can't spell," said Joseph. "Neither can I, but I knew it was wrong, at least."

"And once you know it's wrong, you can always look it up," said Gordon in an instructional voice that seemed to come out of him unbidden. He's tall and thin, and he leans over a little when he talks to you. He's younger than I am.

"I get it mixed up with *desperate*," said Joseph. "Is that *a* too?"

"No, *e*," I said. I hesitated. I didn't remember whether Joseph and I had ever had the next part of the conversation I always have with other people about spelling. "*Desperate* is blue, just that splash of red near the end," I said quickly. "*Separate* is symmetrical—red in the middle, blue on both ends."

"What?" said Gordon.

"Irene is crazy on the subject of the alphabet," Joseph said. "She's been telling me this for years." He picked up the student's paper again and seemed to lose himself in it, as if what I was saying had finally released him. I guess I *had* talked about it before.

"When I picture the letters of the alphabet," I said to Gordon, "I see them in colors. *A* is red and *e* is blue. So a word with lots of *e*'s in it, like *independent,* is bluish in my mind— blue and green, actually. *N*'s are green." I was getting carried away. "That last *e* just *couldn't* be an *a*—there's no red anywhere in that word."

Gordon laughed. "You know what? I see what you mean," he said. "I guess I do imagine letters in colors." He stopped and thought for a moment. "*A* isn't red, though, it's orange. Of course, our color sense would differ." Gordon is black. I laughed.

"But Irene," he went on, in a make-believe shocked whisper, "do you *teach* this?" Gordon and I had never been friends, particularly, and we'd been on opposite sides of an endless faculty debate, all spring, but I liked his voice now.

"I mention it," I said. It comes up now and then, I explained—I find myself saying in class that spelling is easier for some than for others, that if you happen to see the letters in color . . . A couple of students nod slowly and then—always—argue about *which* colors, while the rest of the class smiles indulgently to the left and right, and a few people make little circles next to their heads with their index fingers. Occasionally someone has a more intricate system than mine. "*K* is yellow," this student will say dreamily, "but a *lemon* yellow, not a deep yellow like *u*."

"William James mentions it," I finished. "It's in *The Principles of Psychology*."

"Don't be defensive," said Gordon. "It's interesting. You should write it up." He looked as if he were waiting to see how seriously I took myself.

Now Joseph looked up. "Could you two go someplace else to talk?" he said.

I slapped my forehead to show that I was married to an impossible person, but Gordon apologized. "I've been alone all day," he said. "When I saw the light in here—"

"Is your family away?" I said. He seemed to want to be asked. I'd met Gordon's wife, Judith, once, and they had a cute baby, a girl called Kim.

Gordon said over his shoulder, almost into his bag, almost from out in the corridor, "Judith seems to have left me."

I jumped up to follow him, barefoot. "She *left* you? Are you serious?"

"Fairly serious." He turned back, and I sat down again. "We were planning to spend three weeks in California with her parents, but the other day she told me she wanted to go alone with Kim. She didn't want me to come. They left this morning."

Joseph had put the exam paper down and was listening hard, his head leaning forward on his clasped hands. "This is out of the blue?"

"Well, yes," said Gordon. "Basically. There's been some tension between us . . . but nothing—you know . . . And I get along with her parents better than she does."

"You think she wants a separation?" I said.

"She said she needed to think about us. I don't know what

she wants. Right now, I miss them—and I needed that vacation!"

"Of course you did," I said.

"It's ironic," said Gordon. "I thought now we'd finally have time for each other, a little time off. . . ."

Joseph had put his papers aside and stood up, and he was looking out the window and playing with the cord attached to the shade, his shoulders turned away from us. "You know," he said abruptly, and turned back toward the room, "this cabin Irene and the kids and I are going to has an extra daybed. Why don't you come up for a couple of days? A little vacation at least. . . ." He stopped.

I was astonished, and I think Gordon was too. "Oh, well, look—" he said, and put the bag down to gesture, a quick erasure in the air with his hand. He and I really weren't friends. But he was touched too, I could see. I didn't say anything, but eventually Gordon said he'd come, and they figured out a day, and Joseph wrote down the directions. They just talked over my head.

When Gordon left, I put my sandals on, stood up, and closed the door. "Joseph," I said, still standing near it, "how could you do that?"

"He's a friend of yours—and he's in trouble," said Joseph. "Why shouldn't we give him a little break?"

"I think you invited him only because he's black," I said. "You're so anxious to be the sort of white guy who has black friends, that the minute some black person shows up, you grab him."

It probably wasn't true—maybe hearing about Judith had troubled Joseph. When Joseph and Susan split up, she moved out unexpectedly—she went to visit a friend in New York, and when she came back a week later, she'd been job hunting and apartment hunting there. While I was still arguing, I saw that I wasn't going to let Joseph cancel the visit. But I couldn't stop being angry and neither could he, and we kept talking, and all in all, we didn't get to bed until three that night.

I remember a lesson in the fourth grade. The teacher pulled the shades down, and turned off the lights, and then she sat my best friend, Alexandra, in a chair with a lamp on her lap. The lampshade had been taken off, and Alexandra squinted, and giggled when the teacher said, "You're the sun, dear." Then the teacher carried the classroom globe around Alexandra, and turned it so we'd all see night and day, winter and summer, move across the world.

The cabin in New Hampshire was under pine trees, chilly and dim, but a few steps away was a dirt road in the open, and a field where a horse grazed, and on cold, sunny mornings during those two weeks, I'd take my cup of coffee and hurry to the road in my sweatshirt, and it was like stepping to the side of the globe lit by the teacher's lamp. Feeling the warmth on my scalp through my hair, I'd walk, drink my coffee, and watch the horse. I'd push my sleeves up. There were trees with leaves on the road, instead of evergreens, and they made shadows so crisp you could see the leaves' lobes and notches in their images on the ground. Gordon arrived just after dark one night, and raved about the countryside he'd seen driving up. I found myself thinking that maybe his life had straightened out. I'd been glad to see him after all, but I was pleased when he and my own family slept late the next morning, so I could be alone for those minutes. Gordon had been hunched in his sleeping bag on the daybed when I went out, but everyone was getting up when I came back, and we planned the day.

We wanted to climb Mount Monadnock, about twenty miles

away. But the right-hand turn signal on our car hadn't been working for a day or two, and Joseph said that before we went hiking, he'd drive to a garage in town and buy a new bulb. "I don't want to drive twenty miles without turn signals," he said. He and Gordon were having coffee on the screened porch and I was keeping them company.

"What if it's not just the bulb?" I said. "What if it takes hours?" I was cold again, and impatient to be hiking. Most of the porch was in deep shade, though sunlight touched us here and there. Gordon's left arm, lying along the armrest of his wooden Adirondack chair, was in full sun; it looked long, thin, and dark brown, and he turned it slowly, as we talked, as if to encourage and even out the warming. Joseph stood up, taking his car keys out of his pants pocket. "Oh, if it needs work, I'll just make an appointment to have it done later in the week," he said.

"If you can't get it fixed we can take my car," said Gordon, though his car was small for five.

"Sure," said Joseph quickly, "or we can take ours and I'll use hand signals after all."

Off he went—and didn't come back for three hours. It wasn't the bulb but the relay, and they had to send out for a part. I don't think Joseph even asked for an appointment later in the week. I'm not sure he ever intended to—and I still don't know why. When he got back, he no longer thought it would take a full day to climb Mount Monadnock, as he had before—he thought it would be fine to leave right then. "I don't know what you're upset about," he said to me. "*You* spent the morning here at the lake, not in that dirty garage."

First, that morning, I'd packed a lunch, and Gordon offered to put it into the same bag I'd seen at the college. We stood around waiting for Joseph, Gordon swinging his bag, I all set

in my walking shoes, Tim studying a map and telling us facts
he learned from it—elevations, distances. Then Nicki asked to
take Gordon rowing, and we decided I could wave them in
when Joseph turned up—which wasn't necessary, of course.
They were out there in the boat for a long time while I read
on the porch, being talked to by Tim, and I'd look up and see
them, the boat always turning toward the right, Nicki's weaker
side. Then I heard them land, and they came through the trees,
Gordon carrying Nicki's life jacket, Nicki's legs flashing out
occasionally in little kicks and leaps—but Joseph still wasn't
back. Later Gordon and Tim and Nicki all worked on a difficult jigsaw puzzle they found in the cabin. Gordon seemed
willing to search for straight-sided pieces with my children—
they were putting together the outside rim—and so I excused
myself; I wanted to be in the sun.

As I reached the door, I heard Nicki interrupt herself—she'd
been thinking aloud about whether it made sense to search for
all the pieces that looked like parts of horses—and say, "Gordon, are you glad you're black?"

Gordon laughed. "Yes," he said. There was a pause. "Yes.
Though it has its moments. Are you glad you're white, Nicki?"

"I'm not sure," said Nicki. "I might be glad I'm everything I
am—white, Jewish, a girl—but just because I'm used to them."
They began talking about the puzzle again, and I went outside
and found a sunny rock to lean against. I was rereading *Emma,*
and I'd read a chapter or two before anyone came out. Then
Gordon came up behind me. "I finished the man with the red
cloak," he said.

"How did you stop?" I said. "If I start, I can't stop."

"Oh, I can stop." He crouched down next to me and picked
up some pine needles, letting them sift through his fingers, and
then I stood up, so he stood up. We walked toward the lake.

I wanted to ask whether he'd heard from Judith, and found myself doing so just when I'd decided I shouldn't.

"A couple of times," he said. "It doesn't look good." We were standing on the little sandy beach, right at the edge of the lake, and Gordon dug his shoe into the wet sand and moved his foot in an arc to make a wedge of smooth, damp sand with the pattern of his sole on it. Then he smoothed it over with the same foot, and did it again.

"Kim will have no memory of her parents living in the same house," he said, crouching to sprinkle sand, by hand this time, on a new damp wedge. "What must that do to a child?"

"Terrible," I said, inadequately, but he went on, "Still, there's my brother's daughter—he was divorced, and there were rough spots, but now she's fine. She's going into sixth grade—Nicki reminds me of her, a little."

I looked up at the place in the lake where I'd seen Nicki rowing the boat in circles. There was a canoe sliding past, far from us, but I heard a few words spoken by a woman paddling in the front. *"Even so!"* she said—oddly, almost as if she'd heard us. I turned to Gordon.

"Your brother must be much older than you," I said. "A daughter in sixth grade."

"He married at twenty-one," said Gordon. "He's only two years older."

"My sister's two years older than I am," I said. We were both the younger of two children.

"There are things that happened to one of us," Gordon said, "say around high-school age—and we can't remember which."

"Exactly!" I said, so struck that he laughed.

"Sometimes I think I'll never be close to anyone again, the way my brother and I were," he said.

I turned toward him (I'd been looking out at the lake again, at the glints of light on the water) because of what he'd said, or because I'd heard a noise, and I saw that, beyond him, our car was slowly pulling into the open place under the pines where we usually parked it. I watched Joseph get out and come toward us, stuffing his keys into the pockets of his tan pants. I thought how pleasant it would be if I wasn't going to fight with him, but of course I was. He acted as if we'd agreed all along that he'd stay and have the car repaired, whatever was wrong—and I did fight with him, though it didn't accomplish anything, he just got annoyed. Gordon was embarrassed, of course—he probably thought it was another marriage falling apart. So I stopped yelling and let the others persuade me that there was enough time left to climb that mountain before dark, and Gordon got into the back seat of the car with Tim and Nicki, his knapsack—full of our tuna sandwiches and peaches—on his lap. By the time we reached the state park where the mountain is, and started up, we were all so hungry that we sat down on some rocks and ate lunch right away, though Tim said people would laugh at us, needing to stop only a minute from the start of the trail.

Mount Monadnock gets climbed a lot, and many groups were there—most already coming down, but a few, I was pleased to see, starting when we were. It was lovely, crowded or not. I watched the light sifting through the trees. The trail was wide and clear, and once we got started, we moved along quickly. Nicki didn't whine—to impress Gordon, perhaps. People coming down smiled at us; an elderly woman tripped and almost bumped into Nicki. "Sorry, sis!" she called out cheerfully. "Here comes Grandma the Steamroller!" Everyone was conspiring not to compete at mountaineering—except Joseph, who told me I wanted to rest too often.

"It's not fun unless it's a *bit* of a challenge," he said. Gordon, though, said twice that he'd never climbed a mountain before, and he kept consulting Nicki, who clearly couldn't tell whether he was serious, about the likelihood of avalanches.

Mount Monadnock is bare on top, because of a fire in the nineteenth century, and so the going did get somewhat difficult after a while. The trees shrank to bushes and then they too were gone; in places it was hard to scramble over a rock—and once Gordon swung his bag out as if he were losing his balance, and reached for my shoulder with his other hand. I was keeping Nicki ahead of me, but after that I tried to keep him close too. Joseph and Tim had moved ahead of the rest of us, and occasionally waved and pointed from sunny rocks over our heads.

Eventually we reached the top. It was bright and windy, with views of distant mountains, lakes, and farms, and we sat and stretched our legs and talked to other people up there. I saw Gordon turn aside and take off his shoes and socks, and I could see that he was examining his toes, but he didn't say anything.

The way down was easier. We even met three or four groups coming up, grinning as we all made room for one another on the trail. Nicki was tired, though, and Tim was turning edgy. I thought Joseph might be putting some kind of subtle pressure on him—they were exactly the same height last summer, and Joseph needed to make something of it at times. We stopped to rest where the trees were dense again, and now the light seemed less bright than it had been. I didn't have my watch on. Gordon looked weary, sitting on a log, but he suddenly jumped up.

"I don't have my bag," he said. "I must have left it on the mountain."

I didn't know what to do, but, immediately, Joseph assured Gordon he'd climb back up and find it—almost before Nicki had satisfied herself that none of the rest of us was somehow carrying Gordon's knapsack without having noticed it.

Joseph seemed to assume that Tim would go with him, but Tim said, "Gordon, I'm sorry—but there are heroes and anti-heroes, and I'm an anti."

"Don't be silly," said Gordon. "Of course I'll go."

"No, your feet hurt," I said. Gordon looked sharply at me, as if I'd read his mind, which made me want to hug him. He was attractive, and I saw that I'd been annoyed with Joseph all day partly because he wasn't being irresistible himself, to keep Gordon in perspective. "I'll go—it'll be romantic, just Joseph and me," I said—and realized it was tactless to say that to someone whose wife had just left him, but of course I'd settled the question. The three others headed down the mountain, Tim taking along Joseph's keys so they could wait for us in the car and listen to the radio.

Starting back up, with Joseph close behind me—but somehow not treading on my heels—I felt uneasy. It was late. For the first time that day I thought of the mountain as a natural, even a wild place, where we might be doing something foolish. But my anxieties clarified themselves, and I turned to Joseph. "How could I have *said* that?"

"Said what?"

"That it would be romantic to go with you."

"I didn't mind," said Joseph.

"Of course *you* didn't mind," I said. "*Gordon* minded."

"Why?" said Joseph. "Did *he* want a romantic twosome with you?"

"You're impossible," I said, though I enjoyed his denseness.

But Joseph must have understood me, because he said, "I wonder if he's heard from his wife."

I told Joseph what Gordon had said, and how I'd persuaded myself in advance that everything was fine.

"I knew everything wasn't fine," said Joseph. He was climbing ahead of me now, looking large and solid, wearing a wide brown belt, his wallet making a bulge in his back pocket. I didn't answer—I was trying too hard to keep going. We were still nowhere near the top, though we were back at the low shrubs and bushes, but I was so tired I had to sit down. There was an open place with a big boulder, and I could see great distances.

"I'm exhausted," I said.

"It made me think of Susan," he said, stopping. "Do you want to wait for me here?" I didn't want to, but I didn't see how I could keep going, and so I did wait.

He was gone a long time, and nobody came by in either direction. I didn't know what time it was. I looked out at green New Hampshire, at lakes and towns I couldn't identify, and worried about Joseph—that he'd fall on the rocks and die, or need me to save him. But I couldn't figure out a rescue, and so I forced myself to think about something else. I remembered the morning with Gordon, and Nicki asking him whether he liked being black. It was one of the reasons I wasn't sure what he was thinking, I decided, though not much more important than all the other reasons people are never sure—and then I saw that it was I, not Joseph, who might have wanted to make friends with black people in order to be the right sort of white person. I began a more realistic worry—that Joseph might come slowly into view, but without Gordon's old khaki bag dangling from his elbow, and then I began to feel sure that the bag wouldn't be there, up on top of the mountain, and when Joseph finally appeared, just as I'd begun counting to a hundred a third time, it turned out that I was right. He plopped down beside me and said, "It wasn't there."

We started slowly down. "It means a lot to him, that bag," said Joseph.

"I know it," I said. "It's old." My foot slipped on a twig that shifted as I stepped on it, and I almost fell. Joseph took my hand, but in a few minutes I needed both my hands again to hold back a bush and let myself down a rock.

"Maybe the bag was turned in at the ranger station," said Joseph.

"Maybe," I said, and saw how nice that would be, though unlikely, and not quite as nice as if Joseph and I had found it for Gordon ourselves. I thought we might be getting close to the bottom now, but I wasn't sure, and I was tired and afraid of tripping. Joseph was ahead of me, and I hurried to catch up to him. "Do you know what Nicki said to Gordon?" I said, when I reached him. "She asked him whether he likes being black."

"She did?" said Joseph. "What did he say?"

"He said he does."

"That's good. You know, Irene, I keep thinking about what you said the other night—that I invited him so I'd seem like—"

I interrupted. "I shouldn't have said that," I said.

"Well—because I was going to say—I don't think it's true about me. This morning, when I stayed away, I asked myself if it had something to do with Gordon, or race, or anything like that—and the very idea of it—"

"I know," I said. "You're not like that."

We were quiet for a time. I was looking for landmarks I remembered. Then Joseph said, "I knew the bag wouldn't be up there."

"So did I," I said. "At least, at first I was sure it would be, but then I began to think it probably wouldn't."

"No," said Joseph. "I don't mean that." He stopped.

"Well, what *do* you mean?" I said. I was terribly tired now, and a negative edge to his voice irritated me.

"I mean I *knew*," said Joseph. "I'd seen somebody go by with it while we were resting."

"You what?"

"Well," he said, "it was a few minutes before Gordon realized it was gone. I saw a man go by with a bag on his shoulder and—I can't believe I was so stupid—I said to myself, 'What a coincidence—that bag is just like Gordon's.' "

"But you didn't say anything—I mean even later, when he missed it."

"I was too upset," said Joseph. "And I thought, maybe it *wasn't* the same bag. But I knew it was."

"I can't believe you didn't say anything," I said, stunned.

"I couldn't tell him I'd seen it and hadn't been smart enough to get it back for him," he said. "I *couldn't*. He's my guest— and his marriage is falling apart—and he's *black*."

"You mean you made me climb this mountain twice for *nothing*?" I said.

"That's about it," said Joseph. We walked some more, and I waited to feel angry, but I didn't.

"I would never have done that," I finally said, but still, more in wonder than anger.

"You mean you're too honest?"

I considered. "No," I said. "I'd just have blurted it out. I'd have been upset about making the mistake—but not about people *knowing*. That part's not a big deal to me."

Joseph said, "Oh, is it ever a big deal to me!" It was one of the occasional moments when I'm certain I haven't imagined him: I would never have done what he'd done, wouldn't have dreamt it or invented it—Joseph was, simply, *not me*.

The bag had actually been turned in. Ours was the only car in the parking lot when we finally got there in the near dark. The light was on in the car. We walked up to it, and through the window I saw Gordon sitting in the front passenger seat next to Tim, who was twisting the dial of the radio. The bag was in Gordon's lap—he was running his fingers over the leather strips that fastened the buckles.

Back on the mountain, Joseph had said, "I had to *do* something." He paused. "But I'm sorry. You're very tired." We were silent again, and I thought about how tired I was, indeed, though now I was sure we were near the bottom. "Oh, that *moment*, when I realized the bag I'd seen was his!" Joseph said—as if he were going to tell me all about it, as if he were glad to be talking—but he didn't say much more, in fact, and a little while later, as we reached the place where the path broadened, near the end, I found myself thinking of the time in summer school, a few weeks earlier, when I'd told my class about imagining the letters of the alphabet in colors, and of one student who knew what I meant—a shy, inarticulate girl. The papers she'd written had told me nothing about what she was like, and even that day, when I said my alphabet was in color, and she smiled and kept saying, "Yes! Yes!," the more she thought about what she'd revealed, it seemed, the less happy she was, because she blushed, and shook her head, and piled her hands on her mouth. It was as if she knew she had many secret selves in there, and didn't like to think which of them, next, might make a run for light and freedom.

. . . .

They All Went Up
to Amsterdam

I take Stephen into the nap room and settle him in the right-hand crib. It's the one under the window but I know Stephen will go to sleep without playing with the curtain.

April has finished her bottle and is standing up. I have forgotten Stephen's bottle. I go out and get his bottle from the refrigerator; it's the one with the nipple shaped like a bear. I carry it in. I give it to him. Allison doesn't take a bottle.

April and Allison are making sounds to each other. I drag the rocker down from the other end of the room. It's made of interwoven strips of green and white vinyl stapled to an aluminum frame. I take Allison on my lap so April will not have anyone to talk to. I position the rocker with my back to April so she will not talk to me either. I rock Allison and sing "I've Been Working on the Railroad."

Stephen is lying down but April is standing up looking at me. Allison lies easily against my body. Her eyes are open. After a while I put her back into her crib. I take up April. April starts to cry. I try to soothe her before Allison gets interested.

April sobs. She wrenches off my lap and reaches for a book on the floor. I pick up the book. I sit down in the rocker and April lies back against me. She stops crying. I hold the book so both of us can see it. I turn the pages and say words that fit the pictures: "Bus." "Baby." "Snowplow."

The door opens. Bruce brings Margot into the room. He is leading her by the hand and carrying her bottle, a green pillow, and a book. She is talking to him in a loud voice. April rolls over to look at her.

Bruce gets Margot to lie down on the blue cot next to the wall, just beyond Stephen's crib. He goes out of the room and shuts the door. Margot sits up and tells me to read to her. I have to keep my rocker positioned between Allison and April. If I went to sit on Margot's cot, they would talk to each other. I tell her I'll do it soon. Stephen draws up his legs like a frog.

I rock April. She stares up at me. After a while I see that she doesn't see me. I slip my arm under her thighs and scoop her up. I step to the crib and tip her over into it, lowering her slowly so she is on her stomach on top of my arm. I keep on humming. I hum "I've Been Working on the Railroad." I draw my arm out carefully and hold my hand lightly on her back. I keep it there for a long time. I stop humming but she doesn't move. Her eyes are open but she cannot see. I take my hand off her back. She doesn't move. After a while I step away. Wearily, she pulls herself to her feet and holds on to the railing of the crib.

Allison is lying down with her back to the room. Margot is sitting up with her feet on the floor. Stephen is asleep. I sit down on Margot's cot and stretch her out. I read to her in a low voice. While I am reading, April starts calling—urgently, wordlessly—to Allison. Allison rolls over and calls back. She stands up. They hoot to each other as if they mean something, laughing.

When I finish the book, Margot says she wants a blanket. I find a yellow one. She says it is the wrong one. She wants the puppy one. I find the puppy one and carry it to her. She lies down and gathers the pillow and the blanket and the bottle into a bundle at her chest. I lay Allison and April back down in their cribs and rub their necks and backs and bottoms—first Allison, then April.

The door opens slowly. Bruce's arm urges Nikki and Kara into the nap room. The door closes. I put Nikki on the green cot at the very front of the room, the one on which the fabric is coming away from the aluminum bar at the side. Nikki lies down and plays her fingers along the frayed edge. Allison is standing up.

There is a mattress on the floor near Nikki's cot but if I put Kara on it she would talk to Nikki. She won't talk to Allison and April, who are babies. I pull the mattress down the room and put it near Allison's crib. I guide Kara by the shoulder so she will not stop to talk to Nikki or Margot. I put her on the mattress and smooth her hair off her face. She says she wants a book and a blanket. Nikki calls out that she wants a book and a blanket too. Margot says she doesn't like the puppy blanket.

I give the puppy blanket to Kara and give Margot another blanket. I give Nikki and Kara books. Nikki reminds me about her blanket. I find a yellow blanket. It is a thermal blanket with a satin binding, but it is the wrong one. I know it is the wrong one even before I show it to her. Nikki's blanket has a satin binding but is more faded than this. I go outside for Nikki's blanket. It is on the top of the cubbies. I go back inside and give it to Nikki. Allison is still standing. April is crying a little. I go to her and pat her bottom. Her bottle has rolled to the other end of the crib, where she can't see it. I give it to her. She likes to hold it. She is quiet.

I pick up Nikki and carry her back to the rocker. With my foot, I pull the rocker away from the cribs and Kara's mattress. I sit down and take Nikki on my lap. I rock Nikki. I like the smell of her hair. With my foot, I pull a book toward me along the floor. I reach down for it and read it to Nikki.

Kara says, "I want to hear a book." I say, "Soon."

Allison and April are standing up. When I finish Nikki's book, I take Allison out of her crib and position the rocker between her and April again. I hold Allison and sing "I've Been Working on the Railroad." I sing it three times. When I get to Dinah blowing her horn, I sing, "Allison, blow your horn." When I get to someone in the kitchen, I sing, "Someone's in the kitchen with Allison." Margot sits up and puts her blanket over her head like a ghost costume. Nikki sits up and puts her blanket over her head too.

Next I sing "There Were Three Jolly Fishermen." I sing "fisherwomen," though I have to hurry the syllables. Instead of Abraham, Isaac, and Jacob, I sing Allison, Nikki, and Margot. Halfway through the singing, when the fisherwomen go to Amsterdam, I see April lie down and fall asleep, though I am not looking straight at her.

I put Allison back into her crib, take the blankets off Nikki's and Margot's heads, and lay them down. Margot will not fall asleep soon.

I take Kara on my lap and read her a book and rock her. I put her back on her cot. I lie down on the floor next to her. I rub her thighs and sing "Michael, Row Your Boat Ashore," except I sing, "Kara, row your boat ashore." It is quiet and dark.

Allison is asleep. I hear Margot and Nikki start to talk in low voices so I put the rocker between them and rock by myself, with my back to Kara.

There is a particular way to rock. Though I am alone in the rocker now, I rock in the particular way, pushing a little harder than necessary on the front push and letting the back part of my mind slide slowly out of my head and down the back of the rocker, not caring with the front part of my mind whether they sleep or not, but with the middle part—the slow, certain part of my mind—closing their eyes, easing my mind over eyelids, Nikki's eyelids, easing my mind over the wrinkles in Nikki's eyelids, so that they smooth slowly, rounding over her eyeballs. But then they pull back. I rock heavily and hum and round Nikki's eyelids with the hands of my middle mind, over her eyeballs. Again they snap up but it does not matter. The pull of my rocker takes Nikki's eyelids and smooths them over her eyeballs again. The next time, she is able to open them only halfway. Then she is able to let only a flash of light out of her eyes. Then they are closed.

Margot cannot sleep, will never sleep, unless I forget her. But I hear sounds from the next room and I am tired of sitting here. Still, I must give Margot that present, let her be missing. One person or another is always thinking of Margot, snapping her into response, like someone who must remember how to speak when the telephone rings.

I rock and let the back of my mind leak down, and take the front of my mind and shape it carefully, making it play with what I will do when I leave here—projects for a perfect evening, food, Scotch, something made of smooth, dark-red cloth, someone's hand, all coming to me, all having something to give, something free: steam rising from cooked foods, fingers on my neck and shoulders. When the perfect evening is done, Margot is forgotten and can sleep. She is gone.

There is nothing that can help Kara sleep, now that she is too big to let herself go when her thighs are kneaded and her back is smoothed. There is nothing to do but to lie on the floor and wait. I take a pillow and lie down. I will not sleep; I am wary with wanting what I want. I can think of anything now, but I am wanting what I want. I wait and wait. She fingers the blanket. I won't win. I wait and wait. I'm not going to win. Her eyes ride steadily over the room, conscious, seeing. Impatience grows in me. The back of my mind slips up into place. I want to know what time it is.

Kara yawns. This is different. I hum silently now, for myself—the same song over and over. I know that I've won. I hum for a long time. I use my own name in the song. She arches and sleeps.

Cake Night

Roberta is tearing lettuce leaves—a romaine lettuce and a bright, puckery green-leaf lettuce—and trying to remember when she stopped being in love with Matthew. The short period when they slept together was ten years ago, when Roberta had been married to Toby for eleven years and their daughter, Nan, was eight. Toby knew, at least at the end. Now she has been married to Toby for twenty-one years and Nan is away at college. Roberta rinses the lettuce leaves—she holds the slotted basket under the cold water for a long time, turning some of the leaves—and spins them dry. After she told Matthew she wasn't going to sleep with him any longer, she would run into him occasionally downtown. For hours afterward, she'd imagine— not sex, usually, just talking to him, asking him to dinner. Matthew is younger than Roberta and Toby, and when they had first met—he was a graduate student who took a job painting their house one summer—he had easily become a light-hearted friend of the household who showed up now and then without fuss.

After a long while, he *did* begin to drop in again, and the old tone, amazingly, was resumed. Then he'd bring girlfriends. Did she mind? After a while he met Roberta's sister Molly—who had known about the affair but only moved to New Haven after it was over—and eventually he married her. Now Molly and Matthew have a two-year-old son called Jamie, she is very pregnant with their second child, and they are all coming to dinner.

Roberta is unwrapping a wedge of cheddar cheese and putting a handful of Triscuits onto a tray when the doorbell rings, but then, immediately, the door is opened with a key. It's Molly, who has arrived by herself, and Toby, coming along behind her, just getting home from his office. Roberta calls to them as she takes wineglasses from the cupboard. Their voices come in from the hall; she can hear Molly saying that the others will be along, and Toby asking for her coat, and saying he will certainly hang it up—Molly had said she could just throw it somewhere—and she pictures his supple arm plucking Molly's bulky blue jacket from her shoulders and his hand sliding a hanger into its armholes.

As Roberta carries her tray into the living room, Molly squeezes past her, in bright yellow, and hugs her—carefully, not to upset the tray. "I want orange juice," Molly says.

"Wait, I'll get it for you," says Roberta, but Molly shakes her head and keeps going, and Roberta puts the tray down on a low table in the living room, where Toby is standing, running his hands through his light curls: his coming-home gesture, as if his professional bothers (he's an architect) were gnats and mosquitoes that hummed and buzzed around him until set free.

"I meant to be home earlier," Toby says.

"That's all right." The doorbell rings again, and this time it's

Matthew, with Jamie. Matthew hands his coat to Roberta, then crouches to unzip Jamie's jacket. "Jamie and I had a run-in with the world's most dreadful woman," he says, "but we escaped." He's smiling.

"That's terrible," says Roberta. "Hi." She hugs him as he stands up. Toby has come toward the door to say hello too.

"Hi, hi," says Matthew, shaking hands with Toby. He's shorter than Toby. He used to have a beard. "Is Molly here? I think I was supposed to come straight over instead of going home first."

"Yes," says Roberta. "She's in the kitchen." Roberta gives Matthew a glass of wine. Then she takes two crackers from the tray and puts one into each of Jamie's hands. He stands near her and eats their corners, and Roberta sits down cross-legged on the rug near the table, her skirt bunched under her, to slice the cheese. "Dreadful how, Matthew?" she says—but as she speaks, in comes Molly in her yellow maternity smock, talking to Roberta before she's quite inside the room. "I'm still a wreck, despite your predictions," she says, but then she leans over to let Jamie drink from her glass of juice, and kisses Matthew.

Molly doesn't look like a wreck. She has short red hair, and eyebrows so high and light she seems surprised all the time, and she looks fine as she crosses between Roberta and Toby in funny, baggy brown pants and the cotton smock, the glass of orange juice in her hand.

"I'm still positive it's a boy, and I can't stop thinking about it," Molly says. "I don't want to care. I don't think people *should* care. But this time I want a girl."

"This really *is* bothering you," Roberta says, looking up from the cheese. They'd talked about it on the phone the day before.

Molly sits down on the sofa and drinks her juice, resting one hand on her belly. "But it's a nice boy, I think," she says. "I can feel his foot."

"You really think you can tell it's a boy," Toby says. "What makes you so sure?"

Molly takes her hand off her middle, puts down her juice, and leans back. "It's a boy," she says slowly. "I'm more and more certain. I don't know why."

"Daughters are good," says Roberta.

"Why don't you wait and be disappointed if it *is* a boy?" says Matthew.

"Oh, no," Molly says. "I have to get my disappointment done with." She stretches out a hand and Roberta puts a slice of cheese onto a cracker and reaches it over to her.

"Then again, some pregnant women *know*," Roberta says. She has a cracker in her own mouth too. "Wouldn't that be strange? But listen—eat lots of crackers and cheese, everybody. Dinner's just soup—and dessert, of course."

"But some of them don't let the doctor tell them the sex," Molly says. "Even if they *do* have amniocentesis. I don't think I'd let them tell me, actually. . . . If I were two years older, I'd have had to do that." She is thirty-three, eight years younger than Roberta.

"You wouldn't let them tell you?" Roberta says.

"I don't think so," says Molly. "I need the whole nine months to think about it. Soup and dessert," she goes on. "I need soup and dessert too."

It's Cake Night. Roberta, who is ordinarily a piano teacher, turned away new pupils this year. At times she's worked as a pastry cook, mostly when Nan was small. In those days she baked cakes for a restaurant—surprisingly, Roberta could place smooth curlicues of chocolate perfectly, and make delicate oval petals for the pink frosting roses. She's not usually like that, not careful except about cakes and the piano (and at the piano, of course, there is always compromise), nor able to make things turn out just so.

Teaching, she wished she could place something and have it stay put, unlike her pupils' fingers, which strayed, on purpose or not. This year she bakes wedding cakes for a caterer—tall, lovely white cakes, more elegant than showy, sleekly iced, but with one dark rosebud on top, and a few green frosting leaves. But she takes them to receptions herself, and one day she was driving with a freshly baked cake in a box in the back seat, and when she rounded a curve, it slid onto the floor. She couldn't bring herself to stop and open the box until she'd figured out that if necessary she could hastily bake another cake and deliver it late—though not unforgivably late. In fact, just a little of the icing was crushed, and she had time to go home and fix it. Since then, though, every month she bakes enough extra cake for one assembled wedding cake, and freezes it. So far she hasn't needed it, and at the end of the month she thaws it, spreads frosting on the flat sheets—or doesn't bother—and invites Molly, Matthew, and Jamie to supper.

"Soup will be comforting," says Matthew. "I had a tough day."

"Oh, right—the dreadful woman," Roberta says. "We're sorry, Matthew—you've been trying to tell us."

"Well, it's Friday," Matthew begins. "The day I take care of Jamie." He's been keeping Jamie at his office once a week since Molly took a leave from her job. She's an art teacher in a middle school, but she wanted some time for her own paintings before the baby came (paintings of people and trees, lately, the leaves distinct, the people a blur) and time alone with Jamie too. They'd withdrawn him from his day-care center, but then Molly couldn't paint, so Matthew takes him once a week, and so does Roberta, when she can.

"And I had to go to a meeting in Hartford," says Matthew. He runs a job-training program for poor people, here in New Haven. "The guy who organized it said, 'No problem—bring the kid,' so I did—I thought there would just be a few people, but it was crowded, with some woman making a formal presentation."

Jamie has climbed into Molly's lap. Molly can't seem to get comfortable—she's too big—and she puts him down. "Jamie!" calls Toby softly, and pats his knee, but Jamie heads for the tray of crackers.

"I held him on my lap," says Matthew. "People kept smiling at me—you know, See the Heroic Daddy. Then the woman said she was going to show some slides, and I told Jamie they'd turn off the lights, and it would get dark. I thought he might be afraid of the dark."

"He isn't," Molly puts in. "He was, but he isn't now."

"Whatever. I thought he might be. And so Jamie started saying, *loudly,* 'Dark—light! Dark—light!' " Toby laughs. "He wouldn't stop," Matthew goes on, "and the next thing I knew, the woman said, 'I just can't *proceed* with that baby crying!' " He stops imitating the woman to laugh.

"Oh, for heaven's *sake!*" says Roberta.

"Well," says Matthew, "I wasn't going to hang around and argue with her. I just left. We had to take the train, because we'd driven up with some people, in somebody else's car. I just whispered to one of them that we'd walk to the station, but I got lost, and it was cold. Jamie cried." He looks disturbed, but then brightens. "But he loved the train, didn't you, Pumpkin?"

"Train?" says Molly, leaning toward Jamie. "Did you and Daddy go on the train?"

"Train," says Jamie. "Truck."

"That's *right!*" says Matthew. "He kept pointing out *trucks* we could see from the window."

"I can't *stand* people like that," says Roberta. When Nan was noisy in public, as a small child, Roberta always felt helpless, and afraid of the annoyance of strangers.

"No, no," Molly says, sitting up. "Matthew just didn't think. He was dumb."

"It wouldn't be the first time," says Matthew placidly.

"Everybody knows you can't take a two-year-old to a meeting," Molly says. "You should have told me. He could have stayed home. Besides, he hasn't been afraid of the dark for months."

Roberta has stood up and is on her way to the kitchen, but she pauses in the doorway. "But Matthew couldn't *help* it," she says, suddenly angry with Molly—for not being furious, right away, at the dreadful woman. "That woman was just—"

"She could have been *polite,*" says Toby, but Molly is saying to Roberta, "Wait. Could you decorate a cake with a two-year-old in the room?"

"Yes," says Roberta, although she couldn't.

"Could you play the piano?"

"Oh, forget it," says Roberta. "Let's eat." Toby stands up and motions to the others to go first, and they all move toward the kitchen, Matthew leading Jamie by the hand.

"Yes, I *could* play the piano," Roberta says—she can't stop herself—as everyone else sits down, and she carries a large pot of soup to the table. But then she shakes her head, and starts ladling soup into bowls while Toby begins slicing bread. He pushes the salad bowl in Matthew's direction, but Matthew stands up and goes to the refrigerator.

"What do you need, Matt?" Roberta says—and feels the question quiet her.

"An ice cube," says Matthew, "to cool Jamie's soup." He takes the tray of ice cubes out of the freezer and whacks it on the counter to free one cube. Then he drops it into Jamie's plastic bowl, and sits down, and now everyone reaches for bread and butter, or salad, and dips into the soup—chicken soup with carrots, mushrooms, peas, and escarole. Roberta picks up her spoon. She has always put escarole into chicken soup.

"Your soup still reminds me of Dennis," says Molly, her voice cheerful again. "Remember him?"

"Damn right I remember him," Roberta says. Dennis was a man Molly was involved with in Boston—it must have been around the time of Roberta's affair with Matthew. He was a drummer. Roberta never trusted him.

"I once came to visit Roberta and Toby," says Molly to Matthew. "It was when things were going badly with Dennis—and we had chicken soup. You made so much"—she turns toward Roberta—"that we just ate it all weekend. I kept crying—I picture an empty soup bowl surrounded by used tissues—and you kept saying, 'You don't need him!' "

"And did the soup make you give him up?" says Matthew.

"Well, I gave him up," Molly says. "Obviously. What do I need to give up now, Roberta? Not Matthew, I hope."

"Oh, feeling bad, I guess," says Roberta.

"I know," says Molly. "All day long, I think about little girls I won't have. I don't know why, really."

"It's a good worry," says Toby. "Good worries are better than bad worries." Roberta looks at him. Unborn babies seem fragile. This one is in the room with them now.

"Well, I'm also worried about when this kid will make an appearance," Molly says. "I'm so sick of being pregnant. I wish it would be born. *He. He.* Get used to it, Moll." She lowers her head for the last sentence, to speak sharply to herself, then looks up again. "My due date isn't for three more days, but I feel as if I'm a month late."

"And Jamie was a week overdue," says Matthew.

"Did you think I'd forgotten, Matthew?" Molly says. He shakes his head, and reaches out to touch her arm, and then they all eat their soup.

Jamie, who skipped his nap, gets weepy, and when the soup and bread are eaten Matthew offers to change him into his pajamas, which Molly brought along, and put him to sleep on Roberta and Toby's bed. They can carry him out to the car later. "Good," says Roberta. "I need some privacy here, anyway. You go too, Molly."

Toby begins clearing and scraping dishes, and, once the others are out of the room, Roberta brings pans of cake out of the pantry, and takes a bowl of frosting from the refrigerator. She meant to do this in the afternoon. Usually, when they eat the spare cake each month, she just spreads a simple icing on the flat sheets, but this time she's going to assemble an old-fashioned wedding cake complete with bride and groom figurines on top, a small boy doll, and a little pink plastic baby with a painted-on diaper. As she starts to trim the large layers, Toby finishes what he's doing. "I'll go be a host," he says. "I'll wash the rest later."

"Sure," says Roberta. He watches her for a moment over his shoulder, and leaves the room. Roberta goes back to the pantry for her pastry bag and sets to work. Toby had been right about the woman at the meeting—she ought to have been polite. But in her mind, she's arguing with Matthew. "You brought that on yourself," she tells him inwardly. "You let it happen." It's not what she said before. Once, she and Matthew were in bed in his apartment, and they'd just made love. After a while, lying in his bed, looking out the window at the bare branches outside, she remembered that she had intended to phone him and break the appointment. "I'm not actually here," she had said. Then—seriously—"I didn't want to come." It was true. She'd wanted to be alone that day, and had planned a happy, solitary afternoon. "Why didn't you stay home, then?" said Matthew, puzzled. She'd turned over in bed, away from the window, and raised herself up on one elbow. "You *choose* to do this!" she'd shouted at him. "Well—yes," he'd said.

Yet she must have chosen too. She remembers a long, cold winter walk with Matthew. "We're in love with each other," he'd said. That was the real beginning. She was cold, and she needed to go to the bathroom, and she was in love. Matthew was wearing a worn denim jacket lined with red plaid flannel that showed at the neck, and he had a navy-blue watch cap pulled low over his dark brown hair. That afternoon, walking and walking, Roberta did not let herself reach out and touch his earlobes, just below his cap, or his beard, or run her finger down the orange seam on the arm of his jacket.

One Saturday morning, when she'd been sleeping with Matthew for a couple of months, she got up early and went for a walk alone. It was starting to be spring, but the trees were still bare. When she came home, Toby was in the shower. She lay down on their bed in her jeans and sweater, on her stomach, facing away from the door, and waited. When he came into the room, in his bathrobe, she said, "I have to tell you something, Toby," and rolled over awkwardly and sat up, kicking off her shoes. She faced him. "I've been sleeping with Mat-

thew—not many times—for about two months." Toby looked
at her. "I'm sorry," she said.

He didn't speak for a long time. He stood still, not starting
to get dressed, as if he felt self-conscious about taking off his
bathrobe. "Why are you telling me now?" he'd said.

"Because I'm ready to stop." He seemed to believe her.

"I'm glad it's over," he said. He didn't seem angry, but sad,
as if there were something fresh and young that Roberta and
Matthew had found together—a secret green place, and they
hadn't let Toby in. And now, more than those few afternoons
in Matthew's bed, what seems surprising and worth remember-
ing is how feeling seemed to change the very appearance of
everything that year, the look of air meeting the edges of ob-
jects—of the branches outside Matthew's window, their broken
curves.

There's a streak of frosting on Roberta's sleeve. She scrapes
it off with the dull side of a knife; it will probably stain her
sweater. But the cake is ready; it's in steplike tiers, as traditional as cakes she remembers staring at as a child in a bakery
window. The icing is in sensuous ridges, dipping and rising at
the rim of each tier. On top are the familiar figurines of bride
in gown and veil and groom in cutaway coat and top hat. The
boy doll, somewhat larger than his parents, in blue shorts, sits
at their feet with his legs sticking straight out; and the plastic
baby—of no gender—lies on its stomach on a bed of frosting.
Going to call the others, Roberta glimpses herself in the hall
mirror. She's flushed and smiling, and there's more icing in her
hair.

Roberta is deeply asleep that night—or the next morning, at
about three—after the cake had been laughed over, admired,
and partly eaten, and Matthew and Molly had gone quietly

home, Matthew carrying sleeping Jamie tipped back against his
shoulder, a blanket around him, and Molly bearing leftover
cake wrapped in foil—when the telephone, which seems louder
than it does in the daytime, rings next to her ear. She is frightened, thinking of Nan miles away, but it's Matthew's voice.
"Roberta? I'm sorry. But . . . Molly's in labor."

"Really? The baby? Molly's in labor?" Toby rolls over and
stares at her.

"Could one of you come for Jamie?" Matthew says. "I'm really
sorry. Her contractions are five minutes apart, and her water
just broke. The midwife wants us to be able to get to the hospital on short notice."

"Of course," says Roberta. "We planned that I'd come for
him. Of course I'll come." It seems wonderful to her—not a
bother—that suddenly, in the middle of the night, she can help
bring along this baby, and she gets off the phone and tells
Toby that Molly is in labor and she must go for Jamie.

"I'll go too," he says, sitting up, but she'd rather go alone,
and easily persuades him to lie down again. She dresses quickly
in the clothes she took off a few hours ago.

"I thought that baby would be another week at least," she
says.

She doesn't feel sleepy at all. She kisses Toby, goes down
the stairs, locks the door behind her, and tries the doorknob.
The noise of the car's engine is intrusive on their quiet street,
and she doesn't see another car in motion until she has turned
onto a wider one, and still another. When she stops for a red
light on Whalley Avenue, no one crosses in front of her, and
she stares ahead. Without the usual clutter of traffic, the street-
lights and traffic lights form long straight rows all the way
downtown.

Someone is walking on the green as she drives down Elm,

and then she turns onto Orange Street and drives without another car in sight, thinking about the baby. Matthew lived on one of these streets when they first knew him. During the time he painted their house, they had longer and longer conversations, and when the job was done, he continued to show up—to borrow books or just to talk, leaning on doorjambs or drinking coffee with Toby or, mostly, with her.

One night, all those years ago, she and Toby had been driving home from a party through this neighborhood, and Roberta suddenly looked out the window and thought she saw Matthew walking alone. He turned down a side street, and she asked Toby to turn too. But when they passed the man she saw that it was somebody else. She said, "Oh, never mind—I thought for a second it was Matthew. I just wanted to tell him something, the dope—he convinced me I was wrong about a book last week—but I was right all along." She'd spoken with gaiety, but she could hear an odd urgency in her voice, and a few minutes later, she'd started to cry.

On Linden Street, where Molly and Matthew live, Roberta finds a place to park and rings their doorbell. Matthew comes down the stairs—they have the second-floor apartment in a two-family house—and the two of them tiptoe back up. Jamie greets her at the door, wide awake, in the yellow pajamas he'd had on at the end of the evening, which seems unlikely, somehow, as if it had been days ago.

Then he runs for a shopping bag Molly had filled with his things, and takes Roberta by the hand to lead her downstairs, cheerfully calling, "Bye!" to his parents.

"Hold it a second," says Roberta. She gives Matthew a little hug, and then Molly appears in the doorway, looking preoccupied and grouchy, and Roberta kisses her. Matthew looks happy and follows her to the top of the stairs. Jamie himself is already dragging the shopping bag down the stairs, and Roberta hurries after him.

She drives him home and carries him and the shopping bag up their walk, because all he has on his feet are the feet of the pajamas. When she sets him down on the porch to unlock the door, he seems small and important—they are surrounded by so much darkness—and it is with an air of importance that he climbs the stairs and lets himself be put to bed in Nan's room.

Back in her own bed, Roberta lies awake, alert. First she thinks about Jamie, and then about Molly and the baby, and she begins to remember Molly and Matthew's wedding, a summer wedding, with a reception in their yard, hers and Toby's. It's a small yard, but there were just a few guests, and Matthew laughing, it seemed, all day, his beard trimmed, and Molly in a white cotton dress with a deep flounce at the hem. Somebody else had baked the cake, but Roberta had worked hard anyway, and she was worn out with details of food and flowers by the time the party began—but glad she'd done it.

When the reception was almost over, she went to be with Toby, who was by himself on a bench in the shade. When she sat down, he put his arm around her and eased her against his shoulder; she must have looked tired. Behind her, she heard Matthew talking to her mother—the old, calm goodwill in his voice, and a slight new tension as he began to be a son-in-law. She leaned back and, quieting down, studied the corner of the house in detail (the drainpipe, the brackets that held it in place), and a maple tree just above her. She searched the heavy layers of leaves, the bright and dark greens, searched up, to see how it could be that each leaf, somewhere, was directly in the path of the sun.

But then Toby had said something. He'd said, "You must feel alone," and Roberta had murmured agreement, but she hadn't understood, though now, in the night, she does. She was fine, hearing Matthew's voice, and happy to be fine. "Toby," she says quietly now, and puts her hand on the center of his back, on his pajama top—he's on his side facing away from her. But he's asleep, of course, and soon she is asleep too, and dreaming that she is in an unfamiliar building, in a large sunny room with wooden beams on all sides. There are long parallel oak tables in the room—or counters—and men and women—she too—are working on something, preparing food of some kind. Everything is white or golden, very clean. But Molly and Matthew, in rumpled clothes, come into the room from behind her. One of them has been carrying a small dark suitcase, but when Roberta turns to face them, it has been set down on the floor and they are standing behind it like lost travelers. Though the room is light, Molly is in shadow, and she's wearing a heavy dark dress that falls in wide folds. The front of her dress is in dimness, but Roberta thinks she can just make out that the folds fall straight, that Molly is no longer pregnant.

"It was a boy. He died," Molly says.

Roberta crosses her arms on the wooden countertop, lowers her head, and sobs. Then she begins to think she might be having a dream, because she knows she is in a strange place, neither her own house nor Molly and Matthew's. But a darker thought fights to win in her, that if someone in her real life had told her the baby had died, she might have brought the words—or the knowledge—into the dream.

The phone is ringing. It's light. She is moving the receiver to her face and saying something. "Roberta?" It's Molly. "Wake up. I had her—it's a girl. Roberta, I had the baby."

"You had the baby? When?"

Molly laughs. "About five minutes ago."

"What time is it? It's a girl? Are you all right?"

"I'm fine. We're both fine. She's beautiful. She's right here. It's eight-thirty."

"Molly—" she says. She's crying.

"I think we're going to call her Emily," says Molly. "Do you think that's OK? You liked 'Ellen' better, when we talked about names, but she *looks* like an Emily."

"I love the name Emily," says Roberta, who loves all names and much else just now.

Great Wits

"All your favorite paintings look like teeth," said Anne. "Straight lines, thin people."

"Thin?" said her father.

"Well, there's no fat on a tooth." Her father, who liked paintings from the Middle Ages and some from the Renaissance ("As long as the people in them aren't sexy and don't swirl around," Anne once pointed out), was a dentist.

"*Enamel,*" Anne said out loud. The rest of the dialogue had been in her mind, for she was alone. She was standing in front of Giovanni Bellini's painting of St. Francis at the Frick Collection, a few blocks from Hunter College, where she was a sophomore. The moment—Anne the student standing in front of the Bellini and discoursing with her absent father—happened years ago, in fact, and now when Anne thinks back on it she finds it curious that she can remember a long-gone imaginary conversation this way, when she's confused about more important events back then. Surely, though, that was the year when her family moved to the new apartment—the year of the party.

In the painting, St. Francis was standing barefoot outside his cave, surrounded by boulders. They did look like teeth, at least a little, and the way Anne searched the painted stony ground, anticipating the pleasure of spotting St. Francis's sandals—she never could remember exactly where they were: under his desk, of course—was something like a dentist's eager scrutiny (she almost laughed at what her mind was coming up with) at the moment when detail was about to tell the truth.

Her father, she knew, would have shrugged at the comparison. They both loved this painting, but he scorned most of the art she had come to care for in a passionate semester of art history. Even in this inner dialogue, when she was so witty and quick, she couldn't get him to pay attention. Yet her father, Dr. Katz, carried on a correspondence about Hans Memling with the curator of a museum somewhere, and he belonged to an organization of amateur art lovers whose members took turns presenting laboriously prepared papers. Though he denounced whole centuries of art, he wasn't ignorant or unintelligent—or if he was, that wasn't the problem between them. Anne thought she was always angry with him because he wasn't logical, yet that seemed like a strange reason to be angry.

At about the time Anne stood in front of St. Francis, her father was writing a paper on the Flemish painter Hugo van der Goes, for the next meeting of the club. He was working on it in his study at the new apartment. One of the reasons that the Katzes had moved to a larger apartment, only three blocks from their old one, on Ridgewood Avenue in Brooklyn, was to get this room for him, although they'd also gained separate bedrooms, finally, for Anne and her younger brother, Jeffrey; Anne had been undressing in the bathroom for years. Not that the study had eased the crowding much. It was only an alcove off the living room, and now her father had put so many papers and cartons on the desk that he'd had to set up a card table on which to work.

Anne was at the Frick that day to discuss paintings not with her father but with her mother, who had never been there. Anne had been talking about the Frick Collection at home ever since she was urged to go there by the art history professor, but her mother said she didn't like art museums. Anne had made her mother feel bad about that, even though she herself, wandering through the distinguished old mansion, often spent as much time playing house in her imagination as she did looking at art. Finally, her mother had promised to meet Anne there, on a day when she had to come to Manhattan for an appointment with an ophthalmologist. Then they could travel home to Brooklyn together on the subway. Anne still lived at home with her family, and rode the subway to college and back every day.

Anne had come to the museum early, after her last class. She'd told her mother where to look for her, but now she hurried back toward the entrance just in time to see her mother come in the front door, smiling tensely and standing up straight. Anne had been the taller one for several years now, but she was still surprised whenever she saw her mother all at once, head to toe, and noticed how little she was. Mrs. Katz smiled and came straight toward Anne, and was disconcerted when the guard at the turnstile told her that she must first check her coat—though Anne, too, was pointing toward the cloakroom.

"You found it," said Anne, when her mother finally came through the turnstile.

"I didn't have any trouble finding it," said her mother. They set out down the corridor.

"How were things at the doctor's?"

"He's very nice," said Anne's mother. She had never seen this doctor before.

"Does he think you need new glasses?"

"Yes, but I'm not going to get them," her mother said. "I don't like getting used to new glasses. And they're expensive."

"But if you need them?"

"Oh, I probably can do without them. I'm getting along now, after all."

Anne turned impatient. "Then why did you go to see him— if you weren't going to do what he said? What's the point?"

Her mother was silent. It was not a good start. Anne stopped in front of Vermeer's *Officer and Girl*—the casually elegant soldier, his back to them, and the radiant woman in a fragile white cap. She waited for her mother to exclaim over the painting.

"I've been thinking about Daddy's study," her mother said. "I don't see how we can have all those people in if he won't clean it up."

Anne persisted. She pointed out some of the details in the painting—the elegant design of the girl's sleeves, her happy eyes. It was her third-favorite painting in the collection, but she didn't feel able to say that.

"It's very real," said her mother tentatively.

"But that's not all," Anne insisted, trying to remember exactly what she had learned about it. "Look at it. Just look at it."

"Well, I *said* it's good, Anne," said her mother, who had turned away from the Vermeer.

They looked at several more paintings, but her mother didn't seem much interested, and finally Anne led her to a bench in the Garden Court, with its plants and skylight, and they sat down. "I'm tired," said her mother. Anne was silent. Then her mother said, "How long do you think it will be before the drops wear off?"

"He put drops in your eyes?"

"Of course he did. How could he examine my eyes without putting drops in? My old ophthalmologist always put drops in."

"You mean you can't *see*?"

"Of course I can see," said her mother. "But things are blurry. I'd have told you, but I knew how much you wanted to show me the museum."

Anne tried and failed not to answer. "So if I took you dancing and you had a broken leg, I suppose you'd just dance?" she asked bitterly. "And if I cooked you a meal and you were throwing up—" She held back tears. "How old do you think I am? Three?"

They got up and went to the cloakroom for their coats. Anne's mother put on her coat, shifting her purse from hand to hand, while Anne watched and did not help her, and then when Anne's coat and books came out she shook off her mother's assistance and thrust her arms into the sleeves, yanking hard, though to do it she'd had to let her pocketbook and her pile of textbooks drop noisily to the museum floor. The guard looked at her, frowning, and called, "Miss! Please!"

In Anne's memory, her mother's visit to the Frick Collection comes about a week before her own display of temper at the Forty-second Street Library—that is, a short time after the move and before the party. Anne had been sent to the library by her father to look up a minor fact about Hugo van der Goes, or perhaps about the times in which he lived. The fact had been written on a three-by-five card that was lost, according to Anne's father, when her mother finally straightened up the study herself, in preparation for the party—so the guests, she said, would not slosh drinks on important papers. Jeffrey, by the way, says

Anne's memory is wrong. He insists that their father's paper on van der Goes was written years earlier, and that he himself borrowed from it for a report on a European painter he'd had to do in junior high.

"The teacher had never heard of Hugo van der Goes," says Jeffrey now. "I remember perfectly. She thought I invented him." This can't be right, because then Anne, who is three years older than her brother, would have had to be in high school at the time her father wrote the paper, but this is the memory Jeffrey has.

College students were permitted to consult books that had to be brought from the stacks, and high-school students were not: Anne is sure about that. Anne had used books from the library stacks before, when she'd written a term paper on Socrates in freshman composition. Now she filled out a slip with the title, author, and call number of the book her father had asked her to consult and waited on line. A man accepted slip after slip from the people ahead of her and sent them down in the pneumatic tube—it seemed avid, sucking in the folded papers—to the library workers in the stacks below.

Once she got the book, it would be easy to find the fact her father needed. He was in a hurry—was he presenting the paper that very night?—and he was going to meet her here at the library, on one of the main staircases, in front of the painting of Milton dictating *Paradise Lost* to his daughters.

"I'm sorry," said the attendant when Anne reached the desk. "High-school students aren't permitted to request books."

"I'm not a high-school student," said Anne, who was always being taken for someone several years younger.

"Do you have a college I.D.?"

"Why do I have to show you anything?" asked Anne, who had her I.D. with her, right there in her wallet. "I've seen you

take book requests from a dozen people while I've been standing here, and you didn't ask for one single I.D."

"Well, they weren't high-school students," said the man.

"Neither am I!"

"I'm sorry, miss," said the attendant. "You look young
to me."

"I fail to see," said Anne—but she was starting to cry; *why
did that always happen?*—"what gives you a right to single me
out. Is it just because I don't use mascara and wear high heels,
or something?"

The attendant would not answer. Anne shouted at him.
Someone behind her called out that she was holding up the
line.

"I bet some of those other people *weren't* college students,"
Anne argued. "You just don't know a college student when you
see one."

"If you'll just show me some identification . . ." said the
man. But she couldn't.

Nor could she explain to her father, later, why not. She walked
away, finally. Then, because she'd allowed herself plenty of time,
she had to stand in front of the picture of Milton for forty
minutes before he came pounding up the stairs, his short legs
pumping hard.

"Did you get it?" he said.

"No."

"No? You couldn't find it? Didn't you look in the index?"

"They wouldn't let me see the book. The man thought I was
in high school."

"What do you mean, high school? Why would I send a high-
school student to the Forty-second Street Library?"

"I was smart enough to do it when I was in high school,"
Anne said.

"No, you'd have been too shy. You'd have walked around that big desk three or four times and gone home. Why didn't you show them something to prove you're in college? Don't you have a receipt from the bookstore or something?"

She breathed in and out once, and tried not to speak too loudly. "I have an identification card. But I didn't *want* to show it because it made me mad that he didn't believe me. He didn't ask one other person to show an I.D. I watched for a long time."

He stared at her. He had brown eyes, which seemed to bulge, the whites prominent, when he was perplexed or frightened. "You wouldn't show it? You had it but you *wouldn't?*" He looked at her, she thought, as if she'd begun to take off her clothes right there on the staircase.

"I hope it isn't going to ruin your talk," Anne managed to say.

"I've got to go," he said. "Of course it isn't going to ruin my talk. I don't let little things make a difference. You just can't *be* like that." He turned away. "Tell Mommy I don't know what time I'll be home—not that she's interested, the way she threw away that important index card, as if it were garbage!"

He ran down the stairs, his feet pounding again.

"Tell her yourself!" Anne called after him, but he was out of earshot.

The main idea of the party was that they'd finally moved to an apartment large enough to have a party *in*. Up to that time, even having Aunt Sylvie, Uncle Mike, and Aunt Ruthie, who came every Sunday, was difficult. Anne's mother had to set up two card tables in the living room, with a large tablecloth—it was beige—spread over both of them. Now they had a dining area off the kitchen, and Anne's parents had bought a dining-room table with a leaf. The table was moved into the living room for the party, to which both family and friends had been invited, including friends of Anne's and Jeffrey's. Dr. Katz's two brothers drove all the way up from Philadelphia.

Anne's mother bought a new rose-colored dress for the party. She was afraid to shorten it herself, because it had inverted pleats, so she took it to a dressmaker in the neighborhood, who turned up the hem and, while she was at it, tightened the neckline, which gaped a bit on Mrs. Katz's narrow chest. The bodice had tucks in front, which, Anne had commented, gave the dress more character than those her mother usually chose.

Anne's mother now insists that all the food for the party was brought in, but Anne's memory is that though the platters of cold cuts came from a delicatessen, her mother made the salads herself—green salad, macaroni salad, and fruit salad—along with her specialty, potato pudding. On the afternoon of the party, Anne came home from buying the fruit and found her mother in the kitchen ironing a dress—a different dress, not the rose-colored one.

"What are you doing that for?" asked Anne, putting the bags down on the table and starting to take out the smaller bags of fruit.

"I changed my mind," her mother said. "I decided not to wear my new dress. I don't like the way it looks on me."

"What are you talking about?" said Anne. "There's nothing wrong with it."

"It makes me look as if I'm trying to hide my age. The style is too youthful for me."

"Oh, that's nonsense," said Anne.

"Well, Daddy said so," said her mother. "I tried it on for him this morning."

"Oh. So it was fine until *he* looked at it."

"Anne, don't get sarcastic," her mother said. "He thinks it's the color, or maybe the fussiness on the chest. He used that word—'fussiness.' "

"There's nothing wrong with that dress, Mother," said Anne. "It's simple and it suits you. You tried it on for me before you took the tags off, remember?"

"Maybe it was a mistake to have it altered. Maybe the neckline has a different effect now."

"Oh, it does *not*. You're being perfectly silly."

"Anne, I don't see why you have to yell at me and criticize me about this," said her mother. "It's a very small matter, after all, what I wear." She unplugged the iron and stood it on its mat on the stove top, coiling the wire around the handle. She laid the old dress—it was brown, Anne remembers—over a chair, so she could fold the ironing board. She seemed overpowered by the contraption, and Anne stepped forward, seizing it to put it away in the broom closet, but took it a moment too soon and pinched her mother's finger under its collapsing leg.

"It's all right," said her mother, thrusting her finger to her mouth as a child would, while Anne stood there apologizing— angrily apologizing—and holding the ironing board in front of her like a shield. Her mother stood still for a moment, then carefully slid her outstretched arms under the newly ironed dress, and carried it to her bedroom.

"I may not hang around here," Jeffrey said casually to their father a few hours later. Then the doorbell rang: the first guest.

"Not stay?"

"Well, a friend of mine has something he wants to show me. I said I might come over."

"Something to show you? It can't wait?"

Jeffrey went to answer the door. "I guess not," he called back, looking over his shoulder at his father and Anne.

"Hi," Anne heard him say next.

Anne knew her brother wouldn't really leave, but her father came over to stand next to her, as they waited to greet the first guest, and whispered, "Maybe you should hide Jeffrey's coat. Who is this friend, all of a sudden? He could have invited him. There's plenty to eat."

"Oh, Daddy, stop it," said Anne. It seemed silly to be lined up this way, so she went back to the kitchen, where her mother was frowning with concentration as she measured coffee into a borrowed electric percolator. The brown dress, to tell the truth, was becoming to her. She looked like a very serious person, Anne thought—Marie Curie or someone of that sort, someone who moved precisely and listened to the inside of her mind.

"You look nice," said Anne. Her mother raised a warning finger in the traditional gesture of one who may lose count, but slowly, so she seemed to ask merely for a little pause. "Seven," she said in a friendly, acknowledging voice. She dipped the measure once more into the coffee can. "Eight."

The food was wonderful, everyone was sure about that. Anne spent the next two hours letting people in, showing them the apartment, taking coats, and carrying trays. She had never been so happy at a party—most of the time there was nothing to do at other people's parties and she never knew what to say. To-night, though, she could tell that everyone thought she'd been about to ask a terribly sensitive question or make a brilliant joke when she'd been called away by the doorbell. Everyone wanted her back.

Now and then, she ran through the living room to see her friend Harriet in a lively conversation with someone—Jeffrey, or her father's receptionist, or Aunt Ruthie. Harriet and Anne had been classmates since junior high.

When the doorbell finally stopped ringing, Anne fixed herself a corned-beef sandwich on a single slice of bread, folded over. Not bothering with salad or potatoes, or even a plate, she carried it through the crowded room to a corner where Harriet was now talking to Dr. Katz, and leaned against the back of an overstuffed chair to listen.

Both Harriet and Dr. Katz were eating vigorously while they talked. They had big sandwiches, which they held tightly, close to their mouths, in order not to let bits of coleslaw drop out. They looked a little alike, Anne thought. They were both short and broad, and Harriet, too, had those wide-open eyes with small pupils—her father's were brown and Harriet's were blue—that seemed to be stretching to take in a quick-paced film flashing before them. Her father and Harriet were having an argument.

"The Middle Ages!" her father was shouting. "Of course the Middle Ages. In *particular* the Middle Ages! You don't think it was crazy in the Dark Ages to be an artist, with nobody having enough to eat and Ostrogoths all over the place?"

"But wait a minute, Dr. Katz," said Harriet. "I don't think that's what you meant before by 'crazy.' "

"Of course I know what I mean by crazy."

"No, that's not what I *mean*," she said. "I don't think what you just said fits with what you said before."

"All I said *before*," said Anne's father, with exaggerated patience, "was 'Great art is sure to madness near allied.' " Now Anne began to understand—it was one of her father's favorite quotations, and in fact one of his favorite ideas: that artists are mad. She'd never been able to make sense of it (the art he liked always seemed safely sane) and she had often suspected that he continued to argue the position partly because she disagreed with him. Her art professor had once talked about the subject in class, and Anne had felt relieved when he said that plenty of geniuses were comfortable members of society. Look at Holbein, he said. Or Velázquez. Anne didn't think she was a genius, but it had bothered her to think that the possibility might be closed forever, since she knew she'd never become lonely and strange, turning away from her family or displeasing her teachers.

"Which was when *you* said," her father went on to Harriet, "that the only composition you wrote that the teacher liked was the week you thought you were out of your mind."

"The paper about my grandmother," said Harriet to Anne. "And always before, I've done worse when he let us pick our topics. It was the week she had the stroke, and I was beside myself, driving my mother back and forth to the hospital. Remember, it was the paper I showed you on the train the other day? Well, I was just telling your father I got an A on it. It's the first thing that guy has liked all term. And I just can't figure it out. You know, I wrote it in the waiting room, late at night— it took me about fifteen minutes. And your father says that art and madness— You know, Dr. Katz, I wasn't exactly *mad,* even that night."

Anne had read the paper and had thought it beautiful, but she knew she wouldn't feel easy, either, with success that came unpredictably, without effort.

" 'Great art is sure to madness near allied,' " quoted Dr. Katz again, now to Anne. "It's from Alexander Pope," he said to Harriet. "I read it in college."

Anne, who had been hearing her father repeat the line since childhood, realized she had something important to say, but her mouth was full, and Harriet was already talking. "Besides," she was saying, "I still don't think that was the way they did things in the Middle Ages. In the course I had last spring—"

"The true artist," said Dr. Katz, "cannot control himself. He must practice his calling, at any cost."

"Daddy," Anne finally broke in, "I've been meaning to tell you this for a week. You know what? All my life I've been hearing you quote that line, and it's *wrong*."

"What do you mean, wrong?" Her father looked straight at her.

"I read it. I happened to read it in my Survey of English Lit. course. It's not 'great art,' it's 'great *wits*.' 'Great *wits* are sure to madness near allied.' And it isn't Pope at all. It's Dryden. It's from *Absalom and Achitophel*. It's about the Jews, actually—that must be why you liked it. Except that it's really about England, of course. It's about a rebellion. I was so amazed when I read it. It was as though I found your *slippers* or your *bathrobe* or something in the middle of my English book."

"No, that can't be right," said her father quickly. "I don't remember anything like that. It must be a different line. I know it's from Alexander Pope."

"Daddy, you're just *wrong*. Why can't you just admit you've been wrong?"

"Great wits?" said her father. "That doesn't even make sense. Great wits—people who make jokes? Crazy people don't make jokes."

"No," Anne said. It was delicious to have the chance to explain something she'd learned herself so very recently. "It's a different meaning of 'wits.' It means intelligent people. Great minds."

"Well, I'm sure I never read anything like that," said her father. "Pope meant geniuses—artists. I'm not an artist, Harriet.

I don't have the *privilege* of genius—the freedom. But at least I don't—"

"Well, I'm no genius either," said Harriet. "But I can't stand it that I've tried so hard, and I'm doing fine in all my other courses but I just can't seem to please this man, and then I hand in this thing that's *nothing* and he writes me this love letter in the margins all of a sudden. Now, how am I supposed to duplicate that? Wait for my grandmother to have another stroke, God forbid?"

Alone, Anne thought, she and Harriet could have figured it out—they could work out anything. They'd spent countless long afternoons sitting and talking on Harriet's bed, which was made up as a couch because it was in her family's living room, and falling silent whenever someone walked through the room—quite often the person they'd been discussing, unless they'd been talking about Anne's parents. For hours, as the room darkened around them, they blamed people—in their families, mostly—for lack of logic, for a superstitious refusal to change, for lives made disorderly by constant struggles to reach order for its own sake. When it grew dark, Anne and Harriet would stand up. Each time, they started the afternoon sitting up straight on the couch, with their legs stuck out over the edge, but by the end they'd have slumped down, after the couch had inched slowly away from the wall and its three pillows had collapsed. Then, before Harriet walked Anne halfway home, they'd straighten the corduroy cover, shove the couch back into place, and plump up the pillows and put them back in their row.

"Really," said Harriet to Anne and Dr. Katz now. "It might have been better if he'd hated that paper too."

"Harriet, maybe for once, when you wrote about your grandma, you made some sense," said Anne's father. "I don't know about you, but my kids—always thinking their parents can't teach them anything. Maybe that's what the teacher liked—that you showed a little concern for your grandmother, for an older person."

"Oh, no. I don't think so," said Harriet, not much disturbed.

But Anne, totally surprised, was almost incoherent. "How do you know what Harriet writes? How can you say such things?" she cried at her father. "And that's not what she means. You haven't even been listening. No wonder you think artists are crazy—you can't make any sense yourself."

Now her father shouted. "Here I am having a reasonable discussion with Harriet, and you have to put your two cents in!" Aunt Ruthie, across the room talking to someone, glanced up at them, and so did a friend of Jeffrey's. "You!" her father went on. "You don't even know the meaning of self-control. You have no control over yourself at all—but this is not losing control in a way that makes something beautiful, something for us all to enjoy. What do you do instead? You cry in the library because they make a perfectly ordinary request of you. You yell at your mother all the time. You couldn't even talk to that man in the library—he probably wasn't even a librarian, a man with a degree, he was probably just a high-school gradu-ate himself. You can't keep control of yourself—just like your mother."

"Like *Mother*?" Anne must have spoken loudly enough for her words to be made out across the room, because she saw that her mother, who was offering a tray of pastries to one of the guests, had turned around to look at her.

"Just like your mother," her father said. "Always losing con-trol of herself. She buys a dress in a ridiculous color, designed for someone trying to attract a man—"

"I'm not the least bit like Mommy," Anne protested. "Just

because you make some remark about her perfectly OK dress, she goes out among her guests in some dowdy old thing—I'd *never* do that. I'd never let you get to me like that."

But her mother had heard. Anne knew it, saw it happening, but couldn't stop her flow of words, even though she knew they weren't true, even though she had time, for she had been watching her mother coming toward them, with the tray steadied against her flat brown chest, and looking at their group—the goal toward which she was moving through the crowd—with anxious care.

In all the years since the party—almost fifteen years now—Anne's mother has never dropped the notion that she looked dowdy that night. This, by the way, is the point at which Anne's memory of the party—and of that time in her life—stops. For a long while, she winced when she thought of that period, and tried to make herself think of something different. Later, she would go through the events once again in her mind, unable to stop, returning over and over to what had happened—or to her memory of what had happened. Sometimes she would change things in her imagination, on purpose. She would divert her mother, coming with the tray—would make her turn aside, distracted by greedy Aunt Sylvie grabbing for a sweet. Or she'd change what she'd said—at one time, it became important to have been clearer, to have argued back sensibly to her father. "It's all based on a misunderstanding of Plato," she'd say to him inwardly, "this traditional equation of art and madness." Or, in her mind, she'd defend herself—but affectionately, lightly. "Oh, Daddy, don't you see? When you lose control, you lose it. If it's OK for those artists, it's OK for me."

Lately, when Anne thinks about these events, she's less uncomfortable. She doesn't change them in her mind. She doesn't know why, because they're still painful. Perhaps it's because she has thought about them so many times that she knows when the pain is coming and can brace herself for it. She rather loves them all, the people in the memories—her parents, even herself—though she has no mercy on any of them. She sees that all of them always did everything wrong.

About the Author

Alice Mattison received her Ph.D. from Harvard University and was trained as a literary scholar, although she has devoted most of her career to being a writing instructor. She now runs the Anderson Street Writing Workshop in New Haven, Connecticut, where she lives with her husband and three children.